She's Got Issues

Stephanie Johnson

URBAN
BOOKS

URBAN BOOKS LLC
www.urbanbooks.net

Urban Books
7 Greene Ave.
Amityville, NY 11701

Copyright © 2004 Stephanie Johnson

ISBN 09743636-4-2

First printing June 2003

10 9 8 7 6 5 4 3 2 1

Distributed by Kensington Publishing
850 Third Ave
New York, NY 10022
For store orders call 1 (800) 221- 2647 ext 527

Printed in Canada

Dedication

I dedicate this book to
Francoise Ferguson,
my mother,
my best friend.

Vester's Book 2007
Very good

ACKNOWLEDGEMENTS

I would like to thank my husband, Lyndon B. Johnson, Sr. and our children for supporting me and my passion to write. They understood when I had to sit for hours to complete a simple thought even though it took time away from them. Thank you so much. I love you! Mwah! Mwah! And you too, Tyson.

To one of my dearest friends, Marion "Angel" Hunter: I can't thank you enough for what you have done for me. Adrienne Dean, Lynda Sylvester, Liz Marro, Angel Elliott, Cassie Huber, Clee in Chicago, Carl Ross Jennings, Jr., Fares Awwad: thank you for encouraging me, for reading my draft and giving noted suggestions. Bobby Byrd, Mark Wilson, Trina Dorsey, Shaun Land, Henry Hurt, my brother Lorenzo Ferguson, Darryl Small and Cessy, and Big Nick Moore, Derrick and Terry Roberts, Dawn and Jose Montijo, my sister Ke-Ke, Lilria, Jackie, and good friends Eddie Page, Paducah, KY, Marilyn Grandi, Argentina, thank you so much for your support.

To my Urban Books family, Carl Weber and my fellow authors, it's on! To Martha, who did the editing, thank you!!! But that just isn't enough. I.O.U!!!!

Ju "JuJubean" Joyner, thanks for hooking up the website! You're alright in my book.

After 20 years, I have reunited with two of my childhood friends, Tysha Lockame-Jackson and Tyshel Lockame, of LockaMe Designs, Los Angeles, CA, and I want to thank them for their support on the West coast. We have so much catching up to do, ladies!!! Tysha and Tyshel are twin designers who created an exclusive garment for me and will do more for me in the future. Check them out at www.lockamedesigns.com. And to all of you who stood by my side, and dulled the thorns that the HATERS attempted and continue to attempt to use as a means of deflating my motivation, I thank you for your encouraging words and many prayers.

Now, speaking of HATERS. I can't leave out THE HATERS. This one's for you. Fa, La, La, La La. Uh, Uh, Um.

Let me clear my throat so I can read this to you clearly.

HATER-ADE, THE MANY COLORS
White chapped lips spit purple venom 'bout me,
'cause I drink all of life and ain't never thirsty.
All y'all who front and put on them charades,
ya clearly jealous, rotten like hot garbage,
and glow of HATER-ADE.
It flows red through your eyes,
and wears green on your skin.
HATER-ADE is in your blood,
your colored demon within.
Blue-gray are your days,
no stars for your black nights,
that yellow stripe down your back represents hate,
a coward's spite.
So you bet' not make no more colors
of that there HATER-ADE,
'cause you're gonna mess around, read one of my books,
and see your ass been played.

And if that's too deep for you, try this:
I don't fight, I write! Make me. Please.

Chapter 1
Sweet Dreams

Sinclair and Aliette pulled up in front of the café located on Prospect Avenue in the Clinton Hills section of Brooklyn. Aliette took a deep breath.

"Don't be scared now," Sinclair said.

"I don't know if *scared* is the right word. I feel sad more than anything else because I have to end a relationship with the only brotha I've ever been with who had an eight-inch dick. You wouldn't be so quick to ditch a dick like that either."

"Trick, I don't feel sorry for your ass. You need to give up all the dicks that dip in your shit and get you some Zovirax or something. If he doing you, he doing other bitches. He married, and you getting married. Neither of you should be seeing each other or anyone else. This is the shit that happens when you're a scratch-and-sniff ho. He told his wife, and you better hope she didn't find out that you getting married and tell Wayne because then your shit is gonna be busted too. And I will be rollin', I'm telling you right now."

"Donnie said he ain't tell his wife. She must've either seen us somewhere or one of her friends saw us. Whatever. Let me get in here and get this shit over with."

"Yeah, go on. He's waiting."

Aliette got out of the car, and Sinclair proceeded to pull off. She noticed a car parked on the other side of the street. She cut a slight smile and continued up the street.

On the driver's side of the parked car sat a woman with a baseball cap and sunglasses, and on the passenger side sat another woman who wasn't disguised. Sinclair stopped when she got about a block away, did a U-turn and put the car in park. She watched as the two women got out of the car and walked toward the café where Aliette was supposed to meet Donnie. Sinclair got out of her car and started to walk back to the café.

The two women walked straight to where Aliette was sitting. One of the women was apparently Donnie's wife, because she slapped the shit out of him. Aliette jumped out of her seat and in the woman's face. They exchanged words; hands started to fly and in an instant the two women were pounding on Aliette. Sinclair started to do a slow trot as she filled with excitement. By the time she got into the café, the two women were digging into Aliette's ass real good. The next thing anyone knew, tables were getting turned over, cups and saucers were flying across the room and these girls were getting their fight on. Sinclair took the opportunity to punch Aliette in the face a few times and pull her hair while Donnie's wife had her in a headlock. Sinclair was acting like she was trying to break them up as she hit Aliette. She didn't care if anyone saw her. She just wanted to get hers in.

One of the customers called the cops since the owners couldn't break up the catfight. If it were shown on HBO, people would have easily paid two or three hundred dollars for ringside seats.

It took three policemen to pry the women apart. They cuffed all four of the women, but Donnie's wife, Selena, wasn't playing. She went from cold capping the shit out of Aliette to literally kicking her in her ass.

After being questioned, the policemen released a very fucked-up Aliette and totally satisfied Sinclair. They asked Aliette if she wanted to press charges, and she declined. Donnie's wife started yelling that she would see Aliette again and finish what she had started. She apparently wasn't done kicking her ass, literally.

At that point the officers had no choice but to arrest Selena. She was hyped as hell so they cuffed her ankles because she kept trying to kick Aliette. They put her and her accomplice in the backseat of one of the cars. While the owner of the café gave a report to the arresting officer of how it all went down, Sinclair and Aliette walked back to Sinclair's car and drove off.

"What the fuck was that all about?" Sinclair asked.

"I don't know. Donnie was supposed to meet me here. I left him a message and shit on his cell phone. Maybe she got it instead. Damn, this is fucked up. My face is scratched and shit, and that sick bitch pulled out my hair. And where the fuck were you? It felt like I was getting my ass kicked by all three of y'all. I know I'm not Mike Tyson but I can hold my own. If I didn't know any better, I could have sworn I felt you hit me too!"

Sinclair pretended to be utterly offended. As she massaged her jaw, she said, "What, bitch? Puhlease. If I hit your ass for real, you'd still be laid out. If you were going to see Donnie, Aliette, you should have been more careful. This was his wife you were fighting. Don't you have any regard for that? How would you feel if it were you? How would you like it if Wayne stepped out on your ass? Oh, my bad, you wanted him, and you were gonna get him no matter what. Your selfishness got you a few lumps," Sinclair teased.

They pulled up to Sinclair's and went inside. After they cleaned themselves up, Aliette got some ice and put it on her face while Sinclair began to brush Aliette's hair.

"Damn, she yanked the shit out your hair. I mean you didn't lose much. Well, okay, yeah, you did. You do have a bald spot or two. And damn, your face. . . "

"Sinclair, I get the fucking point!"

As Sinclair brushed Aliette's hair, she thought about how brilliant her plan had been. She knew Donnie and his wife, Selena, from a few years back. They used to go to the same gym. When Aliette told her she was seeing Donnie, Sinclair waited until she had enough facts to mail to Selena so that she and Aliette would eventually come face-to-face. She felt like a rat, but it felt good. This wasn't how she was brought up but that was okay. Her mother would be so ashamed of her for handling things this way, but she wasn't alive to tell her. She knew what her mother would have said: "Sinclair, sometimes you have to look at the situation and see if it's worth the aggravation."

Sinclair would have answered, "It is. This bitch slept with my husband!"

Sinclair put Aliette's hair up, excused herself and went to the bathroom.

She rinsed her face with cold water. She got on her knees and prayed for forgiveness. Her urges for revenge were getting the best of her, and she needed some serious guidance or who knew what she would do next. She went back into the living room. Aliette was on the phone with Wayne.

"No, I'm gonna chill out here for a while. We went to lunch and now we're gonna watch a movie."

Telling him that bought Aliette some time. The swollen scratch marks on her face would've gone down some when she went home. She could explain the remaining swelling as the result of eating something and having a bad reaction.

The alarm was loud, and it startled Sinclair. It was a bright and sunny Friday morning. Sinclair awoke with a sense of relief that she had only been dreaming, that she didn't just witness Aliette getting her ass kicked to high hell, and that she hadn't been one of the women who was giving the ass kicking.

"Thank God it's Friday." She sighed. She got out of bed, got showered and dressed, and was off to work.

Chapter 2
Time to Unwind

"So girl, are we on for tonight?" Sinclair asked as she turned off her computer.

"Hell yeah. You know our sleepovers are the bomb, but I was thinking that instead of ordering food in, we would go out to the club and then come back to your place, just for a change of pace."

"Sounds cool, but I thought you weren't doing the club thing anymore, or at least you haven't since you and Wayne got engaged. Is there something going on that I don't know about?" Sinclair inquired.

"No, just want to do something different," Aliette answered.

Barry's Place was packed. At least five people were valet parking the cars. The line to get in was around the corner. But to get into Barry's you had to have the look, so half the people waiting in line were going to end up disappointed. The bouncers had a rule: Sexy is in; scary, go to the end. It was sad but true—looks meant everything. Still, people were willing to wait in that line and deal with the rules of vanity because if there was any place to party, it was in Brooklyn, New York, at Barry's Place.

Sinclair fixed her jacket as she walked up the stairs while Aliette had already made her way to the front of the line. When Sinclair finally caught up to Aliette, she felt someone staring at her. Not wanting to look paranoid, she ignored the eerie feeling, paid and went straight into the club. Inside, there were three floors with three bars. The top floor featured R&B, the second played jazz, and the third offered reggae. Since the first two floors were packed, they decided to go to the reggae room and get their drinks.

"Ladies, what can I get you to drink tonight?" the bartender asked.

Sinclair said, "I'll have a gin and tonic."

"And you?" he asked Aliette.

"Ah, I'm not sure yet. Can I have a minute?" While trying not to move her eyes off his luscious lips, she thought, *Damn, that brotha is fine as hell.*

"Sure, take your time," he answered as he displayed his beautiful teeth. His smile glistened against his chocolate skin.

Sinclair looked at Aliette like she was crazy. It never took her this long to order. In fact, she normally had a list of drinks she was going to try throughout the night. For her to not have it together lead Sinclair to believe she had some shit up her sleeve.

"Aliette, what's up with you?" Sinclair asked. Aliette turned her back to the bartender and tried to talk without being too loud.

"Would you look at that fine motherfucker? What the hell is that all about?" Aliette asked. "Girl, whatever you do, don't leave me at this here bar alone or I'm telling you, the shit is on. I might have to cool the kitty."

Aliette turned back around and said, "I'll have a Kamikaze and a splash of you."

They all let out a big laugh.

As he turned to fix the drinks, Sinclair said to Aliette, "Okay, heifer, don't start with your ho shit. We came here to have a good time, not turn somebody out. And you're engaged and getting married. You don't need any shit before you go down the aisle. I'm going to the ladies' room. Get our drinks—and only the drinks. I got next."

Aliette reached in her purse for her money and thought, *I'm cool. It's gonna be okay.* But in reality she had butterflies in her stomach and wanted so bad to reach over the bar and squeeze that nice ass he was sporting. As she handed him her money, she couldn't help but place her entire hand over his. She slowly moved it away and looked him straight in his eyes. Somebody was hooked.

"Ja'qazz," someone yelled from the back, "I need you for a minute."

Ja'qazz? What kind of name is that? she thought. *Sounds like* jackass. *Please don't let it be indicative of his personality.* Still, strange name or not, she thought he was fine as hell and wondered how she could get his number.

He looked at her and said, "Thank you for coming to Barry's Place," and walked to the back.

As she grabbed the drinks, she could feel her hands getting sweaty, and when that happened, the panties were next. She proceeded to look for a table but then saw Sinclair waving her over from the far corner. She nodded, confirming she saw Sinclair, and started to walk over.

"Aliette! Damn, girl. What took you so long? I've been sitting here all parched and shit. Tell me you weren't flirting with that bartender. Hot heifer," Sinclair mused.

"No. I just paid for the drinks and started looking for you. Let's toast. To a long-ass week of the same old bullshit and to a weekend of relaxation." *And to Ja'qazz at Barry's, thank you!* Aliette thought.

They tapped glasses, and Aliette slid a book of matches into her pocket. She had managed to get them while she was paying for the drinks. The matchbook had the bar's phone number on it, and Aliette planned to use it soon.

Chapter 3
Oooooooops!

Sinclair's brownstone sat in the middle of the block. Every morning, she would go down to the corner store and get a protein drink but this morning, she had fruit and cottage cheese and Aliette had bacon and eggs for breakfast. It was obvious they had a little bit too much to drink because neither of them was saying shit.

"Sinclair, I think I have a hangover. My stomach feels kind of funny," Aliette slurred.

"Four Kamikazes and a shot of Remy would pretty much give anybody a hangover. Lay your ass down for a while and try to sleep the rest off. And brush your teeth please before you talk to me again."

"Whatever, bitch. If Wayne calls, tell him I'll call him back when I get up."

"Yeah a'ight," Sinclair grunted as she watched Aliette walk toward the couch.

Aliette fell on the couch and closed her eyes. All she could think about was Ja'qazz. *He has to have a nickname—maybe something like Hot Lips or Buncha Bootie—because I can seriously see myself slipping up and calling him a jackass,* she thought. She laughed a little then fell into a deep sleep. When she woke up she noticed she was alone. She got up and went into the kitchen to get something to drink and saw a note from Sinclair.

Al,

*I went to the gym. Will be back around 4:00 or
so. Think of what we can get into tonight. Peace*

Aliette grabbed a bottle of Pepsi and went
into her coat pocket to get the matches with Barry's
phone number on it. She wondered if she should
call to see if Ja'qazz would be working that night or
if she should just let the whole thing go. Wayne
made her perfectly happy. Why was she feeling the
need to start something with this chump? He
probably had women falling all over him daily and
she was just another groupie.

Let's see, she thought, *I could call just to say
what up and tell him I had a really good time at the club
or I could call and let him know that another minute
with his ass in my face, I would have jumped his bones
right then and there.*

"Nah, I ain't gonna call, not today anyway.
I'll give it a few days and maybe by then I'll forget
about him altogether," she said out loud. She put
the matchbook back in her coat pocket. As she went
back into the living room the phone rang. It was
Wayne.

"Hey, babe," he said. "What's up? Did y'all
have a nice time at the club last night?"

"Yup. Sure did. And we're thinking about
going back tonight. A live jazz band is supposed to
be spitting some notes," she lied. She was just
looking for a reason to go back.

"Cool. I'm steppin' out with the fellas.
We're not sure where we're going yet so I guess I'll
catch up with you tomorrow. Love, peace and hair
grease."

"Love you too," she added and hung up the phone.

Now how could anyone not be happy with a man like that? Not too many women had men who understood that a woman needed her space. She needed her time to do what she wanted, who she wanted or to do nothing at all, including her hair.

"Let me get this shit together," she mumbled. "Sinclair should be home shortly. Let's see. What am I gonna put on? I think I'll suggest that we go out shopping and then back to Barry's. I don't know 'bout Sinclair, but I had me a good time."

Aliette laid out some jeans, a sweater and her brown boots. She grabbed her smaller duffle bag and felt for her underwear. The bag was lighter than usual. Then she realized why. She'd forgotten her camera. She decided she would get a shower, drive home and get it. Very rarely did she travel without it, and this would give her a chance to see Wayne and give him a big kiss. This was what she did when she was feeling a little bit off track. The smell of his skin brought her right back to reality.

After she got out of the shower and did her hair, she grabbed her coat and purse and was out the door. She popped in Usher's CD and "U Got it Bad" came on. She blasted the radio and sang out loud, and thought about how she was again in another situation she thought she would never be. She ran into another fine-ass brotha and wanted to get to know him better. She had a man at home, but she didn't care one bit. She was determined to, if nothing else, feel Ja'qazz's lips on hers. She wanted to feel his hands rub her body. She wanted his tongue to taste her from head to toe and have him end up with his face between her legs.

"Damn," she said as she gently gyrated her hips in her car seat. "I bet he eats a mean pussy. Any man who can eat pussy is a keeper. You never know when you might need him."

As she pulled up to the house, she saw Wayne outside with some of his friends. They were discussing their plans for the night.

"Hey, sexy thang. Come and give me some sugar," he demanded. "I miss you, girl. Why you like leaving big daddy home alone? You know I hate sleeping without you."

"Yeah, yeah. You'll be okay," she said as she planted a big kiss on his lips. His lips weren't bad, but he could never seem to use them to their full potential. Oral sex was a big thing for her. If her man couldn't make her reach her climax when he was eating her out, there was a problem.

She said hello to his friends and went into the house. Wayne always liked watching her walk because he liked the way her ass sashayed in her pants. And don't let her have on those panties he liked. The pair that covered her entire ass drove him crazy. He watched her walk into the house, and he noticed something fell out of her pocket. He acted like he wasn't curious, but as soon as his friends left, he went up the stairs and picked it up.

Barry's Place, huh? Nice place, he thought. He put the matches in his pocket and went into the house to squeeze his baby. He tried to sneak up behind her but her senses told her he was coming.

"You better pull to the bumper correct. You know how to do that shit," she teased as she swung around, grabbed his neck and pulled him toward her. "So you miss me, huh, baby? Tell me," she said.

"Damn straight. And he's damn straight right now, so how about a little bit before you go? A quickie. Just enough to hold me over until you come home tomorrow."

She submitted because when it came to the actual act of sex, he was right on the money. They made love and took a shower together.

"What are you doing here anyway? Aren't you still doing the girl thing tonight?" he asked as they got dressed.

"Yeah, we are," she answered. "I forgot my camera, and you know how I am about my camera. It's my eyes into the world we don't see, even if it's in our face. I never leave home without it.

"And your plans for the night would be?" She asked this because she always liked to know where not to go, especially if he was planning to be there. It's not that she was being sneaky. She just didn't want to run into him while she was hanging out with Sinclair. That's how she was. The last thing a woman or man should want to do is crash their partner's party because they might see something that they didn't like. So to be safe, it was good to know which places were off limits if they weren't going out together.

"I told you before, I'm not sure yet. Grant will be picking me up at eight then we'll go get the rest of bros. Don't worry. I'll be a good boy."

I'm not worried. But maybe you should be, she thought. "Get my camera and meet me outside. Thanks, honey."

He went downstairs to get the camera, and
Aliette tried to use the opportunity to call the bar to
see if Ja'qazz was working. When she reached into
her pocket, she didn't feel the matchbook. She
double-checked all of her pockets. It wasn't there.

"Oh, shit. What the hell?" she whispered.
"Where the fuck did I put those gotdamn matches?"

She picked up the phone to call directory
assistance for the number to the bar, but panicked
when she heard Wayne coming back upstairs. She
hung up the phone quickly before he came back in
the room.

"Here you go, baby. You have film?" Wayne
inquired.

"Yeah, yeah, yeah, I think so," she snapped.

"What's up? Why are you acting all fidgety
and shit?" Wayne asked.

"Nothing. I just remembered that I was
supposed to pick up some dry cleaning for Sinclair.
I gotta go. I'll talk to you later."

She grabbed the camera and her bag and was
out the door. When she got to the car she opened
the door and immediately looked for the matches.
They weren't in there either.

"Damn it! Now I definitely gotta carry my ass
back to Barry's, and this time I'll get Ja'qazz's home
phone number."

She immediately called Sinclair and told her
what their plans were for the night. They would hit
the mall then have a nightcap at the club.

Chapter 4
Close Call

The night was calm. Not that many people were out. All three rooms were evenly occupied so Aliette lead the way to the reggae room. She made it her business to walk by the bar to see if Ja'qazz was working, and lo and behold, he was. So that she didn't seem too anxious, she didn't go straight to the bar. Instead she suggested they find a table then have the waitress bring them their drinks. The table they had the night before was available so they took that one.

They weren't seated five minutes before the waitress came over. "Hi. I'm Janice, your waitress. What'll it be for you girls tonight?" she asked. Knowing that their heads were a bit tight from the night before, they both settled for Kendall Jackson Chardonnay. Janice took their order and headed up to the bar. She told the bartender what they wanted as she pointed in their direction. That gave Aliette the opportunity to be seen by Ja'qazz. Janice came back shortly with their drinks and advised them their tab was paid for by the bartender. She pointed to Ja'qazz. They both raised their glasses in gratitude, and he winked in acceptance of their thanks.

Aliette made eye contact with Ja'qazz. The need to do him was even greater. Imagining his tongue running down her stomach and onto her thighs distracted her.

"Yo!" Sinclair shouted. "Earth to Aliette. Where the hell are you? I asked you how your day was."

"I'm with you, girl. Chill. It was cool, very relaxing. How was your workout? Did you work out for me too?"

"No, I didn't. You need to get into the gym with me. I could use some company, you know."

"I know. My New Year's resolution is to do that just for you. I promise."

They sipped their drinks and enjoyed the music. The deejay put on the strobe lights as it started to get crowded. This was good. Now that there were more people, Sinclair would be distracted and not too inquisitive when Aliette excused herself to go see Ja'qazz. And that was what she did.

"Sin, watch my purse and camera please, girlfriend. Thank you!"

"Yeah, right."

Ja'qazz saw her walking toward him and asked the assisting bartender to cover for him. Sinclair watched Aliette as she made her moves on Ja'qazz. She had leaned back to sip her wine when she noticed Aliette's camera on the seat. She picked it up and focused on Aliette walking.

"Snap," she said with a grin as she pretended to press the button. *Imagine that. She would be caught in the act*, she thought as she drank some more wine. She hung the camera around her neck and acted as if she was getting into the music.

As Aliette got closer, Ja'qazz leaned over the bar and waited. She got close to his face and stared at his lips, then at his eyes, then back at his lips.

"You are so damn fine," she said as she shuffled from one foot to the other. "And you are making me so wet."

Sinclair looked over and saw they were talking. She lifted the camera and took a picture then she went back to enjoying the music.

"Is that right? How you doing tonight? Where's your girlfriend?"

"She's over there, sitting down." They looked over and saw Sinclair snapping her fingers and moving her head to the music. They turned back to each other, and Aliette whispered in his ear. "Can we go in there?" she asked as she pointed to a door that led to a back room.

"For what?"

Sinclair looked over at them again and saw Aliette bend over and whisper something else in his ear.

Okay, this is perfect. I got that bitch's number, she thought as she lifted the camera again and snapped another shot.

"You want to what?" Ja'qazz asked.

"I want to feel your lips," Aliette responded.

"Actually, I do want to talk to you, but promise you'll be good."

She laughed. "I promise," she said as she took his hand and led him into the room. Sinclair took another swig of her wine and saw them heading toward the back room.

Bingo. She snapped a third picture.

Ja'qazz opened the door and went in, and Aliette followed.

Bam. That was flick number four. The film wasn't finished, but she didn't care. She popped it out and put it in her purse. Hopefully Aliette would get so drunk that she wouldn't even notice the film was missing. The first thing in the morning, Sinclair would get the pictures developed.

"Mm, mm, mm. Sometimes things just fall into your lap when you least expect them. We'll see how Wayne will like these pictures."

The room held two couches, some plants and a full bar. It was dimly lit and very comfortable. A big-screen TV set it off just right.

"So to what do I owe the honor of you coming back to Barry's for a second night in a row?" he asked.

"To be perfectly honest with you, when I was here last night and saw you, I was immediately attracted to you. I tried not to show it in front of my girlfriend because, well, you know how they can be, but she picked up on it anyway."

"And?"

"And I wanted to call you but misplaced the matches I got from the bar so I figured I would come in person and get your phone number from you. I hope you don't mind."

"I'm flattered, and I had hoped to see you again because I wanted to ask you something about your friend."

She moved closer and asked him what it was he wanted to know. She could feel the chemistry between them and was sure he felt it, too, but that was not why he pulled her in there. To Aliette, though, it seemed clear from the beads of sweat running down his neatly groomed face that he was just as excited as she was. She moved even closer — so close she could feel his breath. She closed her eyes and let her mind take her on a wishful thinking roller-coaster ride that he would have her panties swimming in the moisture from her pulsating pussy. She imagined their bodies would touch and he would have her on the couch, pants off, doing what she loved, tasting her juices. She imagined it would be like nothing she had felt before.

"So, Aliette, about your friend, is she seeing anyone?"

She didn't answer and her eyes were still closed. He was standing in front of her. Her head rolled to the side, and she bit her bottom lip as she backed up and leaned against the door.

"Um," Ja'qazz said.

She was still on her roller coaster and she was ascending to a high point. It was bumpy and her body softly jerked, but she loved the ride so far.

"Wait a minute," she said seductively.

"Aliette!" he yelled.

"Yes! Yes! Yes!" She reached the high point. Her body became still then she let go. She descended into an orgasm that went through a loop, upside down and another two loops before she came to a full stop and was aware he was talking to her.

Ja'qazz looked at her like she was crazy. "You know what? I need to get back to the bar. I'll check you later."

She had one of those orgasms that left her kind of bent to the side, legs quivering. She looked like she was about to fall over. He reached for her and helped her over to the sofa.

"Oh yeah. What school did you learn that from? I need to send them a thank-you card."

He stared at her while he responded. "What are you talking about? I agreed to come in here because I wanted to ask you about your friend Sinclair."

"Oh, my bad! I must have faded out for a moment. Wasn't I standing before?" She laughed while she collected herself. "Whew, it's hot in here. Okay. I apologize for that little episode. Can I tell you what I just did?" She got back up and started to walk toward him again.

"If you must," he said as he stepped aside and away from her. He was getting annoyed.

"I just had one of the best orgasms from imagining what it would feel like if you ate—"

"Aliette," he interrupted her, "I'm not eatin' nothin' of yours. You're a trip. Better yet, a freak. I'm out." He reached for the door and opened it.

"Well, wait. What did you want to talk tome about?" She hung on to his arm and attempted to touch his face softly. He turned his head then walked out. They were near the bar area, and she was still hanging on to his arm.

"Wait. Where are you going?"

"Did I say something that gave you the impression I was feeling you?" he asked.

"What?"

"You heard me. I thought you could get me in with your home girl, but I see how you do."

"What? Nigga, if you wasn't feeling me, you wouldn't have came in this room with me. You know you want some of this."

"You got issues."

"Whatever, fool." She let go of his arm. He walked away. Aliette looked over at Sinclair then went back into the room and slammed the door.

"Motherfucka. He knew damn well he was smelling it. Humph, we'll just have to see how long he can play hard to get."

She primped her hair. The bar was well stocked so she took a bottle of Jack Daniel's, opened it and gulped a few times. She fixed herself up. She hoped Sinclair wasn't getting antsy. Maybe Sinclair hadn't noticed how long she'd been gone. Actually, Aliette had only been gone a few minutes, though to her it felt like much longer.

Aliette checked her reflection to make sure her makeup wasn't smeared and made her way back out to the table where Sinclair had been sitting. But now Sinclair wasn't there. She was on the dance floor. As Aliette got close she started to laugh because Sinclair was having a good time. As she got closer, she thought the guy Sinclair was dancing with looked really familiar. He was familiar. It was Wayne. Sinclair was dancing with Wayne

What the hell is he doing here and how long has he been here? she wondered. She looked around. *His whole fucking crew is here, chilling and shit.* She didn't know if she should act surprised or mad, so she just waited to see what his response to seeing her would be.

After the song was over, Sinclair and Wayne came off the dance floor. Because they were laughing, Aliette assumed there was no problem. To her surprise, Sinclair appeared to be okay, so Aliette chose not to say anything.

"Well, this is a pleasant surprise. What are you doing here?" she asked Wayne as he sat at their table.

"What am I doing here? I thought I would join you out. A friend of mine works here, and since he doesn't get off until midnight, the rest of us thought we would come here and have a few drinks until he gets off. Then we're going up to the city," he explained.

"Which one of your friends works here, and how did you know this was where we were gonna be?"

"You dropped matches from the club when you came to the house. I took a chance and came here hoping to find you. Ja'qazz works here."

"Who?" She wanted to be sure she heard him correctly.

"Ja. His boys call him that. Why are you asking me all of these questions?"

"I just wanna know. Is that alright with you?" she snapped.

She sat in the chair next to Sinclair. Her camera was in the middle of the table and the cap was off.

"You moved this?" she asked Sinclair.

"Yeah. When I saw Wayne and his friends come in, I moved it so that they could sit."

Aliette just looked at Sinclair as she placed the camera back in her bag. She couldn't believe what was happening. Why tonight, of all nights, had Wayne shown up while she was out? And since when were Wayne and Ja friends? His name was never mentioned in her house, and Ja had never called the house.

"So, where were you?" Sinclair asked Aliette.

"I was up at the bar talking to Ja," Aliette answered quietly so Wayne wouldn't hear her. "You know, I'm ready to go home. Are you ready?"

"No. Not really. We just got here. And you're a lying bitch." Sinclair made sure to say it loud enough to get Wayne's attention.

"What? What are you talking about? I was up at the bar. And what I gotta lie to you for?"

"Yeah, okay. I saw you go into that room. I don't know who you think you're fooling. Are you going to live and die as a ho? And you don't lie?"

"I ain't lied to you, Sinclair."

"Ever been married?"

"No!" Aliette looked at Wayne, who kept his mouth shut and waited to see how Aliette would answer. "Yeah." She changed her answer. "What the fuck does that have to do with what we're talking about?"

"You never told me you were married before," Sinclair said.

"Well if your nosy ass must know, I was married. There's a lot you don't know about me."

"And your point is?"

"Now I feel funny, okay?" Aliette said.

"Why you feel funny?" Sinclair asked.

"'Cause you over here accusing me of doing something wrong at the bar and calling me a liar. I can't help it if Ja hit on me when I went up there."

"Bitch, you don't feel funny. When did he hit on you?"

"When I went up there to say hello. He invited me in the back room because he said something about wanting to ask me something. When we got in there, he was looking at me all googly eyed and shit. He started sweating when I asked him what he wanted."

"So? Since when does sweating mean someone is hitting on you? You got issues."

"You know what? I'm tired of you always trying to minimize the fact that I get attention from men, okay? It ain't my fault you don't, or can't. You can take your pick on which reason it is. You jealous."

"Jealous? I'm jealous of you? You right. I'm jealous because you can't seem to be in a committed relationship. I'm jealous because you have no idea who you are and look for validation by sleeping with everything that has a dick. You right, I'm jealous. Oh, have you ever had a threesome?"

"Don't be trying to play me out in front of my man. You're trippin'. You need to stop playing."

"I ain't playing!"

Aliette didn't respond. All she could do was look at Wayne to see what his response was to what Sinclair had said.

Wayne sat in silence while his fiancée and her so-called best friend argued about who was jealous of whom. But he couldn't help but hold on to something Sinclair said. He stared at Aliette while he played it over in his head.

I'm jealous because you have no idea who you are and look for validation by sleeping with everything that has a dick. . .Have you ever had a threesome?

"Well, I'm out," Wayne said as he and his friends got up. He left without another word to the two women.

"Thanks a fucking lot, Sinclair. Why you always gotta start shit?"

Sinclair shrugged and grabbed her purse. "Now I'm ready to go."

Chapter 5
What's Going On?

Aliette stared out of the window while Sinclair drove back to her house.

Tomorrow, I'm gonna take this fucking film down to Wal-Mart's one-hour photo and get this shit developed. They don't show too much of anything but it'll be enough to ruffle Wayne's feathers, Sinclair thought.

She got a lot of nerve pulling my card in front of Wayne. How could she sit there and tell him I fuck everybody? Trifling skank, Aliette thought.

"Why would he come to Barry's?" Aliette asked.

"How the fuck do I know? All I know that you ain't hardly ready to get married to him.

You know, after Donnie I thought you had done all your dirt and was ready to settle down. You're so fucking lucky his wife didn't find out. I've seen that bitch in the kickboxing class at the gym. She would fuck you up! And I wouldn't do shit."

"I know. Tomorrow I'm gonna call Ja and apologize."

"Apologize for what?"

"Girl, when we were in the back room, I was thinking about fucking him so bad that I literally closed my eyes and had a fucking orgasm. It was good too. My shit was hot."

"What? Did you fuck him?"

"No. And that's the thing. If I can cum by just thinking about a man, then you know when he fucks me, he's gonna tear my shit up."

"Why you lie, then? You are such a liar." Sinclair shook her head in disgust.

"You think I was gonna tell you this shit in front of Wayne? Girl, please." Aliette sucked her teeth. "But wait, it gets better. He got mad, girl."

"Mad at what?"

"Mad because I had an orgasm and he didn't get none."

"Yeah, right. That's one thing I can't stand about you. You lie too much. I never know when you're telling the truth. And you lie good sometimes. You better be careful who you lie to."

"Please. Everybody lies, and besides, it's harmless. I'll apologize tomorrow."

That sounded good.

Check her out. She's always trying to put me down. It's all good, though. I'm gonna go see Ja, alright, Aliette thought.

When they got home, Aliette went to take a shower while Sinclair checked her messages. There was one from Wayne.

"Sinclair, give me a call when you can talk in private."

She deleted the message.

Sinclair was tired. Her week at work had been long, and it felt like the weekend had taken forever to get there. She had worked a few hours overtime and hadn't slept much. Now she flopped back onto the bed and laid still. *Me, jealous? Picture that shit. Who would want to go around fucking just to know they exist? Not me. I ain't the one. Jealous? Yeah, right,* she thought.

A few minutes passed then she got up. She took off her clothes and put on her robe.

Aliette was sitting in the bathtub filled with bubbles and she was blowing them in the air when there was a knock on the door.

"Al, you alright? You been in there for a long time," Sinclair asked.

"Yeah. I'll be right out."

She climbed out of the bath, wrapped her hair so that she could dry off, threw her T-shirt and shorts on and went into the living room. Sinclair had turned on the television, but since it was a nice night out they decided to sit on the porch and have girl talk.

"Well, soon you'll be a married woman, girl. You'll be tying the noose right around that skinny neck of yours. I never thought I would see this day. You are the most scandalous woman I've ever known, juggling two and sometimes three men at a time. One might have thought you were single and shit."

"Girl, please. Men have been doing this all of their lives. They can't hate us for learning how to be a player from them when they would leave us home, have us blowing up their pagers and missing in action for days at a time. Hell yeah I cried when that shit happened to me, but when I got tired of the bullshit, I took notes, learned the lesson and walked.

"When I was alone for a while, I gathered myself and decided I wouldn't be any man's shit rag ever again. I would date and keep it on my terms. When I need you, I will call you. If I don't call you, don't call me. The dating scene was cool for a while, and I had my men, all for different reasons, but they all made one man in the end. I needed a complete man, and since I couldn't find one, I had several who made him up. Now that I'm marrying Wayne, my subscription to *How to be a Ho* is expired."

She had a look on her face that wasn't too convincing. Sinclair could tell there was something else going on, so she pried a little more.

"I don't know who you think you foolin'. You're not telling me something, and I wish you would just spit the shit out. I can see there's something else on your mind. Have you heard from Donnie?"

"Okay, but you have to promise me you won't go off. And no. Donnie is old news."

"Go ahead."

"Last night at the club when I excused myself, I was going over to the bar to say hello to Ja'qazz with full intentions on taking him in the back and fucking the shit out of him. He said he wanted to ask me something, but I didn't think it was that important. We were standing close, and I smelled him, his breath. He was sweating, and that shit turned me on. Before I knew it, I had closed my eyes and was thinking about how good it would feel if he had my legs on his shoulders eating me out. I tried to snap out of it but you know how I am with that."

"You dreamed, or whatever, of him eating you out right there in front of him?"

"Yup. Sure did. And I was feeling him bad. I wasn't trying to snap out of it. Anyway, afterward when I got myself together and came back to the table only to find Wayne there, I was kind of taken back."

"Why? He is your fiancé."

"Because, girl, I was trying to get my freak on and he messed my whole mental."

"What does that have to do with anything?"

"You heard him. That's his boy."

"I don't believe that. They may know each other from Barry's, but I don't think they're cool like that."

"Maybe, maybe not. All I know is that I felt weird about it and wanted to leave. But no, you had to go on one of your tangents and try to play me out."

"Well, you know, Aliette, maybe if you had been cheated on, you would know how it feels. That shit is no piece of cake, and it gets on my nerves how you just don't care about how you fuck up somebody's life. You're selfish is all I'm saying."

"I'm not selfish. I just look out for me. But anyhow, I told Ja'qazz what I had done, and like I said to you before, he got angry."

"Well, Aliette, not everybody has sex on their minds twenty-four/seven. There are other things to life. Let me ask you this: Does he know who you are? Does he know you're engaged to Wayne? Really, though, what difference does it make?"

"What do you think? If they're friends, wouldn't you think he would know about me? Oh no. What if this was a test? What if Wayne is testing me because of my past, as a way of seeing if I'm true to him and in love with him before we got married? I did cheat before."

"If that's true, so what? You didn't actually do anything this time, so I'm not sure why you trippin'. Unless you trying to hook up. Is that what you're trying to do?

Aliette just looked at Sinclair. She shook her head and laughed at her. *Who does she think she is, trying to analyze me when she ain't nowhere close to having a man? She been playing this pick-and-choose shit forever, and all it's gotten her are cold and lonely nights in her bed, alone.*

"You know how it is, maybe. I'm about to be married. I want one last dick. Is that so bad? But then I think about how I really want to not do that to Wayne. But then I think again and know how I am. I love da dick!"

"You just a tramp, and I accept you for that," Sinclair said. "Maybe you should come to terms with it as well. Think about it, you cheated on him how many times? You have a problem with being faithful to anybody but yourself."

Aliette laughed; Sinclair didn't. Yes, they were friends, and yes, they talked about things that friends talk about, but Sinclair really thought Aliette was ruthless and couldn't care less about anything or anybody but herself.

"You better hope the day doesn't come when somebody gives you a taste of your own medicine."

"Girl, please, you don't have to worry about that."

Sinclair sat in deep thought. *Wayne has no idea how scandalous this bitch is. Oh, I gotta call him back, and when I do, I'ma let him know. I don't know how I'm going to bring it up, but he will know.* She looked at

Aliette. *I'm not worried, but maybe you should be.* "I know girl, I know," she finally said.

Chapter 6
The Beginning

Mondays were the worst. Sinclair was sitting at her desk typing. She was finding it hard to concentrate because she was feeling very uncool and disturbed with Aliette. Sinclair knew Aliette's ho-ish ways would eventually surface and lead to her cheating on Wayne again. After all, Aliette had a good man who gave her everything, yet before she was to marry him she was daydreaming about another man licking her snatch. This infuriated Sinclair. Every day she thought about the moment she learned of her husband's infidelities.

That's it, she thought. She felt someone had to teach Aliette a lesson. She thought long and hard about what she was about to do, weighing all the options and consequences of her actions. Could she look at Aliette with such great disdain and consider her friendship true?

The phone rang. It was her boss.

"Sinclair, why don't you take the rest of the afternoon off? It's slow, and you've been working so hard lately. You deserve some free time."

"Thanks," Sinclair said. "I will."

"Boy, perfect timing." As she grabbed her purse she decided she would go have a drink to mull over her thoughts and try to figure out the best way to stick up Aliette's ass. Since Barry's was close, she went there. Traffic was light so it only took her about five minutes. When she pulled into the parking lot she noticed Alliette's car was there.

What's this bitch doing here? she wondered.

She fixed her makeup just in case there were some decent men there and went in. As she walked upstairs she heard Aliette's voice doing that *oh, please fuck me, I'm free* laugh. She looked over, and lo and behold, Aliette was hanging all over the bar basically fucking Ja'qazz with her words. Sinclair's blood was boiling but she had to get it under control. She wanted to call Wayne and tell him to come down to the bar and let him see for himself that his woman was still up to her old tricks and still very active in her profession of ho-ology.

"What are you doing here?" Sinclair asked.

"I'm just relaxing, trying to wind down," Aliette responded.

Ja'qazz didn't say anything. He started to clean up the bar.

Yeah, I bet. Wind down into his bed, you stank bitch, Sinclair thought. It was at that moment she decided to go ahead and blow Aliette out of the water, but she needed to get her strategy together so that it was foolproof. Then she would come with both guns blazing. The only thing was Wayne would be crushed. Still, she felt he had to know he was about to marry this woman who definitely wasn't marriage material.

Sinclair sipped on her drink quietly. While Aliette did her thing, Sinclair plotted. She thought she would slip away to call Wayne and ask him to come there and bust her. No. That would be too cut and dry. *That sounds good, though*, she thought. Sinclair wanted to watch Aliette go through the drama she had put and continued to put people through. Let her experience the feeling of hurt, being dumped for another woman or man. Let her feel the anxiety of not knowing where her man was and the gut- wrenching feeling that she was going to shit all over herself when he didn't call her back. Yeah, she really needed to know how that felt.

Sinclair stepped out of the bar and called Wayne.

"Hello." He picked up the phone before the first ring was finished.

"Hey, Wayne. It's Sinclair."

"What up, girl? Whatcha doing?"

"Sitting at Barry's, having a drink. What you doing?"

"Sitting here doing nothing. I called you the other day because something you said bothered me."

"What? What's up?"

"I don't know if you slipped or what, but you basically told me that Aliette still cheats on me whenever she gets a chance. Is that true, Sinclair? Does she still sleep around on me?"

This is your chance. Don't clam up now, she thought.

"Can you come down to Barry's now so we can talk?"

"I guess. It'll take me a few minutes."

"Okay. I'll be here for a while."

They hung up, and Sinclair stood outside the bar and thought for a moment.

There's no turning back now. He can see for himself, and I won't have to actually say anything. An innocent bystander, that's what I'll be. Oh, and I can give him the roll of film.

"I'm sorry, Wayne," she said out loud.

Sinclair went back in the bar. Aliette had moved and was sitting on top of the bar, hanging on a pole that separated two barstools. Ja'qazz was still wiping down the counter and washing glasses. He really wasn't paying too much mind to her. Aliette would say something and he wouldn't answer. He'd just look up and shake his head.

"Aliette, what's up with your girl?"

She ignored his question and changed the subject.

"Hello, I know you hear me," Aliette said as she tried to reach over the bar to tickle him.

"Don't do that," he said. "You gonna hook me up or what?"

"Oh, whatever. And no! Are we ever going to be alone?" Aliette asked as she looked at Sinclair as if to say, *Can a sistah get a moment, please?*

"You referring to me?" Sinclair asked as she took her seat. "'Cause I could give a shit. I came here to have a drink, not see you do your jacked-up rendition of *Coyote Ugly* on the bar."

A while later the door opened and Wayne walked in. Sinclair turned around, saw him coming, then turned back around and didn't say a word. Aliette was trying to reach over to tickle Ja'qazz again when he said, "I thought I asked you not to touch me like that."

"Why you trying to fight it? You know you want some of this."

"Some of what?" Wayne asked.

Aliette turned around so fast she fell off the bar. She stood, brushed herself off and acted like she wasn't cold busted.

"Hey, Sin."

"What's up, Wayne? How you doing?"

"Great, just great. Thank you very much for asking." Wayne looked at Sinclair with both gratitude and hurt in his eyes. She invited him down to Barry's so he could get the answer to his question, and Wayne clearly understood.

"Hey, baby. Um, what are you doing here?" Aliette asked.

Funny, that's the same question I asked you, you clearance rack item, Sinclair thought.

"Girl, call me when you're free," Sinclair said as she got up. She gave Wayne a hug and slipped the roll of film into his jacket pocket.

"Develop that and call me if you want," she whispered in Wayne's ear then left.

"I was just riding by and saw your car. Thought I'd join you, but thanks, I'll pass." He turned to walk out. Aliette called out to him. When he didn't answer, she grabbed her belongings and ran after him.

Wayne proceeded toward his car. Aliette grabbed his arm to stop him.

"Wait."

"For what, Aliette? Oh, I'm sorry for interrupting your little fling."

"Fling? You crazy. Ja'qazz and I are just friends."

"You're lying."

"I'm lying? No, maybe you're the liar. The other night, didn't you say you guys were friends? I never heard you mention his name before. What's that about?"

"You don't know all my friends, Aliette. And I don't feel like I know you, either."

In reality, Wayne and Ja were never friends. He just knew Ja's name from going to Barry's. Something told him to go the bar that night. He had a gut feeling Aliette was still up to her old ways.

"And I can say the same; you don't know all of mine," Aliette told him.

"Well, I guess you're right. I'm going home. Are you staying or what?"

"No, I'm not staying. I'll meet you at home."

They each got in their own cars and left.

It was early evening and Sinclair wasn't in a rush to go home.

"That was some funny shit," she said to herself. As she drove, she couldn't help but fall into deep thought remembering how her life was destroyed, day by day, by some ho who couldn't walk away from a married man, her husband. It was just over a year ago when she noticed a change, and things weren't adding up. At first, she didn't think anything of her husband, Vernon, leaving the house for an hour or so when she got home. He was a journalist, so she figured it was because he had to drop off articles to clients. But when the hour became hours, and after the hours became nights, she hired a private investigator.

After two months of waiting, she received an envelope in the mail. Already knowing what it was, she poured herself a few glasses of wine before she opened it. Finally, feeling quite nice, she slowly slid the letter opener across the seam. She paused, took a deep breath, pulled out the pictures and saw her husband fucking some bitch while another was eating her out in their bedroom. She couldn't believe her eyes. She looked closer at the pictures to see if she knew either one of the women. She didn't, but that didn't relieve the feeling of deceit, hurt and humiliation that overcame her.

Who are they? Does he work with them? she asked herself.

Adrenaline was making her heart feel like it was going to pump right out of her chest. As she fell back on the couch, she was too numb to cry. She closed her eyes and remembered all of the signs. He wasn't coming home for days and sometimes a whole week. The money was off a few times too.

"How could I be so stupid? How could I be so naive?" she wondered out loud.

She opened her eyes and looked at the pictures again. She loved this man, and he was out there sticking his dick in other women. He was exposing her to diseases and who knows what else. She took vows for life but how could she stay married to this motherfucker after this? No. She couldn't let him or the heifers involved get away with this. She had to decide how she was going to handle it.

After days of pondering, she decided she would send a copy of the pictures to one of his most important clients. A week later he was fired. Then she found out who the women were and that they were both married, so she sent copies to both of their spouses. She put the originals in another envelope and mailed a copy to herself, at which time she confronted his loser ass.

As soon as he came through the door, she rushed him.

"What the fuck?" he yelled.

She threw the envelope at him and as he stood there, she paced the floor.

"Open it, motherfucka!"

"Sinclair, I tried to tell you I wanted to take our sex life to another level, and you didn't want to. You never responded to me. Sinclair, please," he pleaded after he opened the envelope and examined its contents.

"Vernon, I don't want to hear the shit. There is nothing you can say that will tell me that those pictures are lying. You've been lying to me for so long. And so what if I didn't want to? That's reason enough for you to go and do it anyway? Cheat on me, Vernon?"

"How was I lying? I told you I was with clients. And I was. Sinclair, what else was I supposed to do?"

She looked at him with unreserved disgust. "You sound dumber than I feel. You jackass, we're married," she yelled. "So you're saying they're clients? Who are they, Mrs. Monday and the half-price special? Fuck you, Vernon. Get yo' shit and get the fuck out!"

Although he tried to come up with every excuse in the book, she couldn't handle his lying. For the first time, none of his lame-ass reasons were good enough.

For days after, she cried. She cried while she was in the shower and she cried herself to sleep almost every night. She didn't eat for days and took two weeks off work, finally realizing that regardless of how much she loved him, she had to cut him loose. In the back of her mind, she knew she deserved more and was worth more, but it was hard for her to feel that way when she was looking at pictures of her husband having sex with not just one, but two other women.

The following weekend he moved his things out. She kept the house, and they split the contents in it. Her days were black. She didn't answer the phone because she knew it was Vernon calling, and to speak to him would only deepen her depression. Her trust in anyone was nonexistent. Therapy didn't help, and neither did medication. It only suppressed her anger, so she stopped both because she couldn't take it anymore.

She decided to go back to school to try to take her mind away from Vernon, and started visiting her mother's grave more. Her mother had died when she was younger, and if she ever needed her, it was when all this mess with Vernon went down. It always made her feel better to go visit her mother's grave. She hadn't been there in a long time, but she knew what her mother would say in this situation.

"Baby, a man is a man, and you will never change how they think. And if you're lucky enough to get one to love you for you with all your faults, you are truly blessed. There is someone out there for everyone."

Dating was out of the question because she was still dealing with finding out about her husband's infidelities. She wasn't over it, not nearly. She often sat in the park and just watched the people live their happy lives, running with their dogs and wrestling with their children while inside, she felt the loneliness one feels when she puts all of her love into someone only to be humiliated.

On one particular day she was sitting on a bench letting the sun sink into her skin. All of a sudden she broke down and started crying hysterically, openly and whole-heartedly. She could hear her surroundings, but there was a sound that was louder than all of the laughter and voices. It was a clicking sound. She looked up to see a woman taking her picture. She didn't know whether to tell the woman to go away or just let do her thing. She wanted to say something but she didn't know what. The woman took a picture of her tear-drenched, puffy-eyed face then introduced herself.

"Hi, my name is Aliette. Aliette Pearly."

Sinclair just stared at her and said nothing. She couldn't help but feel she knew this woman from somewhere.

"Damn, sistah girl. What has you like this? Is it that bad? Can't be any worse than the mess I just got done with. Can I call someone for you? Are you here alone?"

Sinclair was still staring as she picked her brain to figure out where the hell she had seen her face before. School? No. The gym? Uh, no.

"Oh shit," Sinclair whispered. *Oh shit. Oh shit. She's the bitch who was in the picture with Vernon.*

"What'd you say?"

"Say this is not happening. Say that I'm not sitting here crying in front of one of the reasons for my misery."

"You're miserable? That's obvious."

Sinclair didn't answer Aliette.

"Hello? Can you hear me talking to you?" she asked Sinclair, who could hear her voice, but it was like the teacher's voice on the *Peanuts* cartoons. Her words weren't making it to where Sinclair was able to process what she was saying. All Sinclair could think about was how she had to control herself enough to let this thing ride out without giving away who she was. She had to restrain herself to keep from kicking Aliette's ass.

Kicking her ass would mean it's done and over with, Sinclair thought. *That would be too quick and too easy.*

Sinclair had decided it wasn't enough that she had sent copies of the pictures to all those involved, because she only knew the result of her own situation. She believed this day was happening because she still had the hurt inside of her and she needed to be rid of it. She needed to let this chick, who had now come into her life once again, know that what she had done: She had wrecked a household and ruined a marriage.

"I'm okay. I'm just having one of those days. I'm Sinclair. Sinclair Welch." She had to remember her maiden name quickly, because if she used her married name, Aliette might have put two and two together.

"Do you come here often to cry and release yourself? Because I can tell you other ways you can relieve the stress you may be feeling and you may actually enjoy it," Aliette said with a devilish tone in her voice.

"Come with me if you want. I need to finish this film then we can go and talk." They walked over to a group of children. Aliette snapped a few more pictures, finishing the roll of film, then they went to a coffee shop right outside Fort Greene Park.

Aliette ordered cappuccino with a splash of Kahlua.

"And what about you, miss?" the waiter asked Sinclair.

"I'll take a coffee, light and sweet," she replied.

"So, like I said, my name is Aliette and thanks for letting me take your picture. Believe it or not, as a freelance photographer, I never get a chance to take pictures of true feelings like those. If the photo comes out like I think it will, I'm going to enter it in a contest. Well, with your permission, of course. And girl, whatever it is that's got you crying in the park can't be that bad. Try getting a divorce. Even when you ain't got shit, the other person still tries to make it hard as hell."

Sinclair was sipping her coffee and looked into Aliette's eyes. She saw they were vacant, as if she had less than half of a soul.

"Do you come to this park often? I ain't never seen you here. I'm here almost every weekend taking pictures, trying to take the one that will land me in the most prestigious galleries in the world. I don't have it yet."

Does she ever shut the fuck up? Sinclair wondered before she answered.

"No. I just needed to get away from my normal routine. Sort out some things. You know, clear my head," Sinclair answered, still in disbelief she was sitting directly across from the woman who was taking her husband's dick like it was hers.

"Well, maybe we can get together another day. Maybe take in a movie or go for drinks," Aliette suggested.

"Yeah, maybe. Give me your number and I'll call you."

"Okay."

That was six months before, and the beginning of the end of Sinclair's wretchedness. She'd kept it together while befriending Aliette. She was going to ride out the wave.

Chapter 7
Laying Down the Dirt

Sinclair had been home only a short while when the phone rang.

"Hello."

"Sin, it's Aliette. What are you doing?"

"Nada."

"Could you believe that shit that happened today?"

"Yeah, that was pretty wild. What ended up happening?"

"Not a damn thing. I don't know who he thinks he is, popping up where I'm at."

"Let me remind you, he is your fiancé."

"I'm just saying, how did he know?"

"You don't listen very well. So worried about you, you, you. He said he saw your car."

"What the hell is your problem?"

"Ain't my problem. You just think it's always about you when it isn't."

"You know what? I was calling to let you know that I was gonna go back to Barry's to talk to Ja'qazz. I was gonna ask you to cover for me if Wayne called you looking for me, but don't worry about it. I'm not sweating it."

"You haven't had enough, have you?"

"I don't want to hear this shit. I'll catch up with you later."

Sinclair heard a click in her ear. She looked at the phone in amazement. "This bitch has lost her mind."

She went into her bedroom and as she pulled out the photos of her ex-husband performing his ménage à trois, she felt her blood flowing in slow motion. Everything around her took on a fuzzy look. Before she knew it tears were bursting out of her eyes. It was a silent cry, full of fury and despair. The lump in her throat stopped her swallow midway. Her breath paused, and she let out a chest-pressing rasp of a cry. She went into the office area of her bedroom, tore off a piece of tape and taped the picture with the three of them right in the middle of her mirror. The picture was now puckered from her tears.

"Fuck. I could cut her throat!" she said out loud.

She had managed up to this point not to show her feelings and pretend she didn't know Aliette prior to their meeting in the park. She didn't know how much longer she'd be able to do that. She'd have to get her revenge soon.

The bar was empty. Aliette ordered a glass of wine and was waiting at the bar for Ja'qazz when her cell phone rang. She looked at the caller ID and saw it was Wayne. She let it go to her voice mail. She really didn't want to talk to him right then because not only would she have had to explain where she was, talking to him would mess up the feeling she had going on. Anticipation alone had her juices flowing as she thought about those lips and that tight ass.

"Whew." She released a sigh. "He could get it for real." As she sipped her wine, she looked at her watch. She'd been sitting for about ten minutes and hadn't seen Ja yet. The cooks were in the kitchen, the hostess was at the door, but he was nowhere to be found. Finally, she got up and asked the hostess if he was there.

"No. He left about a half-hour ago. You just missed him."

"You didn't see me waiting at the bar?"

"Yes, ma'am. I saw you sitting there but I didn't know you were waiting—"

"Forget it. Thanks for nothing."

She went back to her chair, grabbed her purse, threw the rest of her wine down and walked out with an attitude. She immediately called Sinclair.

"Hello," Sinclair answered in a sleepy voice.

"You sleep?"

"Who is this?"

"Aliette. What are you doing sleeping? It's still early. You sick or something?"

"No. I was tired so I took a nap. How did your little rendezvous go, ho?"

"Be quiet. I don't know why I even bothered with this mess. I'm getting married in a few weeks, and this bullshit should be the last thing on my mind. Did Wayne call?"

"No."

"Alright. I'm on my way home so no need to cover any longer. I'm going to see my man."

"What are you going to say when Wayne asks you where you've been? You know he's going to."

"I'll say I was here talking to you about stuff. I don't know. I ain't worried about him. He gonna be a'ight."

"Before you go home, come over. I want to talk to you. It will only take a few."

"Okay, see you in two."

Sinclair got up and went to the mirror where she had taped the pictures of Vernon. She stood motionless for a few minutes then sighed with angst.

I was so stupid, she thought as she put her head in her hands and gently massaged it. *Loving him made me blind.* She went into the bathroom, brushed her teeth and pulled her hair back. She fixed her bed and fluffed her pillows.

About five minutes later, there was a knock at the door. It was Aliette. Normally she just walked in, but not this time. Sinclair thought that was weird, but went and opened the door.

"Go help yourself to something to drink, if you haven't already had too much."

"No, thank you. I kind of had my fill from these last few days. You know, I don't know what I'm doing."

"Tell me something I don't know," Sinclair said.

"I love Wayne and I'm about to be his wife. I just met Ja'qazz, and I'm jeopardizing my relationship only to be stood up by him. Girl, come on. You are supposed to be my friend. Smack me or something. Tell me that I don't need to be out there like this and that I need to get my shit together."

"Funny you should say that. I wanted to talk to you about this whole thing. I know you must be very nervous about settling down and tying the knot again. I know because I've been there. But if you truly love someone, that's exactly how you should feel. Now, I was thinking since you have a little bit of curiosity left in that cat, we should give you a chance to sow your oats for the last time. What do you think about having a weekend bachelorette party? We could rent a limousine so we don't have to drive, reserve rooms so we don't have to come home, and party, girl. I'm sure Wayne won't mind. In fact, I bet he would love to be a fly on the wall."

"Ooh, girl, that sounds like a good idea. We can go and buy some outfits so we can look cute as hell. Go get our feet and nails done and cut the fuck up. Okay, so when?"

"You're getting married, so let's make it the week before because you know the men will be doing their thing the weekend of the wedding."

"Sin, look, I didn't have the chance to thank you for being a good friend to me. We've only known each other for a short time, and I really want to thank you for putting up with my bullshit, covering me when I was creeping on my man, letting me be myself and not judging me. Thank you so much for doing me the honor of being my maid of honor."

They gave each other a big hug. Aliette went home and Sinclair got in the shower. She took a deep breath as she thought about the situation.

Step one is done. I set it up and now all I have to do is think of what I'm going to do next. Now, I need to find out her deepest secrets and her freakiest fantasies. How can I get this information? We've been friends for a little while, and all I know is that she used to smoke a little weed back in the day. What better way to find out than to ask her directly? She won't think anything of it. She'll think I'm gonna set the mood with one of those things, not actually make them happen.

After she finished taking her shower, she dialed Aliette's number and left a message for her.

"Al, listen, I was thinking. When you get a chance, write down the things you want to do but have been afraid, or haven't had the right opportunity to do, but would love to do before you get noosed. Later. I'll talk to you tomorrow."

"Sinclair." Wayne picked up the phone before she could disconnect the call.

"Hey, Wayne."

"I developed the film. I can't believe it."

"Believe it, Wayne. I'm sorry."

"Don't be. Thanks, Sinclair."

She hung up the phone, crawled into bed and got a good night's sleep.

The next morning flew, and it was almost lunchtime before Sinclair even glanced at the clock. She wasn't hungry, so she figured she would take a walk down to the mall and do some shopping. While she was walking she saw a fitness store and thought she could always use some new shorts or socks, so she went in. She browsed the shorts on the clearance racks then went over to the socks. She grabbed two packs of ankle socks then went over to the sports bra rack. She skimmed through them and stopped at one that was red and black, her high school colors. As she grabbed it off the rack, she heard the bell to the entrance door ring. In came Ja'qazz.

The other day at the bar, she had been too preoccupied with Aliette and never even spoke to him. *Hmm, that wasn't nice,* she thought. Besides, looking at him now, she could see why Aliette thought he was so hot. Sinclair hung the garment back on the rack and approached him.

"Excuse me. Don't I know you from Barry's Place or something like that?" she asked.

"Yeah. I'm Ja. Ja'qazz Johnson," he replied.

"I know. You're all I hear about. I'm Aliette's friend, Sinclair. My friends call me Sin. Nice to meet you," she said as she extended her hand. He took her hand. *Wow,* she thought, *nice grip.* "Do you work here, too, or are you just browsing?"

"No. I needed to buy a new pair of sneakers."

"I see. Well, I'm on my lunch hour, and we all know that an hour is never enough, so I better get going. See you around."

"Well, wait. Um, do you work around here?"

"Mm-hmm. I work right up the block at The Little Printer on Vanderbilt Avenue."

"Can I walk you back to your office?"

"I wasn't going right back. I was gonna pick up a green tea and sit on a bench, but you're more than welcome to join me, I guess." She was trying to play it cool, but Sinclair wouldn't mind one bit if this fine brotha spent some more time with her.

"Cool," he said as he held the door open for Sinclair.

And a gentleman. I like, she thought as she led the way out.

Chapter 8
Tea Time Turns Touchy

The breeze was whimsical and the conversation was stimulating. Sinclair would stare at Ja then when he turned and looked in her eyes, she became almost hypnotized. Being the windows to the soul, she was immediately drawn into his eyes. He actually held good conversation and seemed like he would have something to offer a woman if he found the right one.

"So, what do you do at your job?"

"I format ads for various companies. We don't do big jobs. We primarily cater to the smaller companies because we don't have the staff to take in big jobs. Every now and then we'll do a wedding, but they're few and far between. It's a nice, relaxing atmosphere, and I go home stress free. I get paid good money and get the best perks ever, like going home early and big bonuses and security. The company is family owned so there are only about fifteen people who work there. We have a good time."

"Not too many people speak that highly of their jobs. You're lucky. . .and so are they."

Sinclair couldn't help but notice his eyes were very inviting. They told a story. What story, she wasn't sure. The moment of silence was so loud they were both mesmerized by it and each other. It seemed as though they could hear each other smiling inside.

"Will you look at that? My lunch is up," she said as she looked at her watch. "It was nice talking to you. I'm sure I'll be seeing you around."

"Thank you. I enjoyed myself as well. Take care, and I'll see you later."

She walked away and could feel he was staring at her so she turned around. That was something she never did. And he was staring. His look was strong and serious. It was like he wasn't finished having tea. As she stood there, he got up and started to walk toward her. She sort of shuffled her purse around so she could try to cover up the anxiety overcoming her. She felt kind of tingly, a feeling she hadn't felt in a long time. When he finally reached her, he again told her he really enjoyed talking with her. Then he asked for the second time if he could walk her back to her office. She thought about it for a moment and decided she was going to go with this and see what happened. Surely he couldn't be interested in her other than on a friendship level, but this might be good for her game plan.

"Could you excuse me for a minute?" she asked as she turned back around and dialed the number to her job.

"Hey, it's Sinclair. I ain't coming back this afternoon. I'm feeling kind of weird and think I need to lie down. If you need to reach me, call me at home . . . Right. 555-1379. Otherwise I'll be in tomorrow morning. See ya."

Sinclair turned back around, right into his beautiful, berry lips. The sweetness of his aroma made her legs weak, and she gave in very quickly and slipped him her tongue. It had been such a long time since she even kissed a man and here they were in broad daylight, working up a sweat. As they pulled away from each, she asked, "Want to go somewhere more private so we can talk some more?"

"I'd love to," he responded.

They walked back near the print shop and got her car. He went to get his car and followed her. She peered through her rearview mirror and thought about what had just happened. She hadn't planned it, but these things didn't just happen. She felt it was meant to go just how it did. She could've kept walking and not turned around. She didn't walk away when he started to walk toward her. Instead, she stood there waiting. To top it off, she didn't pull away from his lovely lips when they touched hers. Instead she tongued him down like he was a double chocolate ice cream cone. She had to admit, the feeling was great.

I forgot for a minute what it felt like to be horny, she thought

She shot him a smile when she looked at him through the rearview mirror and he did that slanted grin and winked at her. She drove to a park that was more private and secluded. There was hardly anyone there, which was good, and since she had the rest of the afternoon off, there would be no time constraints. They got out of their cars, both smiling. Ja saw a bench and steered her toward it. They sat in silence for a moment.

"I really don't know what I'm doing here."

"Why we gotta have a reason? Can't two newfound friends chill out and talk about whatever without having a reason?"

"Newfound friends? You're seeing my girl-friend on the down low, but you and I never formally met. I saw you in a fitness store and when I realized who you were, I approached you to say hello. Now here we are. I feel like I already know you."

"Yeah, here we are. There's nothing wrong with that. So, how long have you known Aliette?"

"We met about six months ago at a park. I was sitting trying to catch some sun and she was taking candid pictures of the people. I happened to be one of them. She told me something about me caught her eye and that she had taken a few pictures of me. We got to talking, went and had some coffee and have been friends ever since."

"How close are you guys?"

"We're tight, I guess. I don't necessarily agree with a lot of the shit she does, but who am I to judge? Look, what just happened with us a few minutes ago?"

"It's not that serious. Relax. It was just a kiss."

Sinclair looked at Ja'qazz and playfully rolled her eyes while sucking her tongue through her teeth. She could tell he was very interested in her. Why, though? Wasn't he content with whatever purpose Aliette served for him? *He is scrumptious, though. I could see having him on the side if I needed something extra that I wasn't getting from home. Not that I'm getting any.* Her thoughts were interrupted when he reached over and grabbed her hand.

"What are you in deep thought about?"

"Did you know that Aliette is Wayne's fiancé?"

"Wayne who?"

"Wayne Grieg. You know, your boy."

"No. I don't think I know him."

"I figured as much."

"Why are you asking me that?"

"Never mind."

"No, tell me."

"It's really nothing. It has nothing to do with me. I just wanted to know since you were feeling her."

"Feeling who?" Ja asked as he pulled away.

"Aliette."

"I'm not feeling her. Your girl's a freak."

"You should know that."

"What do you mean I should know that?"

"Now I'm stupid. I know all about you and her going into the back room and —"

"And what? I went with her into the back room. This part is true, but nothing happened. I started to ask her about you, but then she sort of dazed off and shit. I had to help her sit down because she was about to fall over. I wanted to get to know her friend. You. I never got a chance to ask her about you because after I helped her, I thought it was a good time for me to leave. I ain't want her getting all touchy- feely."

"So then what was she doing when I came there and she was having drinks, hanging all over you?"

"She's always trying to see me. I guess she's a nice person and all, but I'm not interested in her. I was — and am still — interested in you. It sounds like your girl would have shortchanged you if given the opportunity. What did she say happened?"

"That you were hitting on her."

"She's a damned liar. You need to check your girl. And you said you guys were friends. Are you sure?"

As Sinclair sat and listened to him, his voice faded and her mind drifted to the pictures she had of her ex-husband and Aliette.

This bitch was trying to cut my legs out from under me again. I ain't no fool twice, and she thinks she could treat me that way and get away with it for a second time? she thought. *She a tart for real.*

"Alright, so you're not interested in her. Since when have you been interested in me?"

"When I saw you sitting at the bar that night. The way your hair fell on your shoulders was very sexy. The way you licked your lips after you took a sip of your drink thoroughly turned me on. At that very moment, I thought about how your skin would feel against mine. I wanted you. I want you now."

Sinclair didn't know what to say. For sure, her juices were flowing like a river running wild and her nipples were firmly pushed against her bra. He knew she was turned on. She daringly moved closer and took him by the chin. She pulled him to her and she kissed him. Then she let him go and got up.

"You know where to find me if you want more of this."

"I do? Where?"

"The print shop on Vanderbilt."

Again, she could feel him staring at her as she walked away, but this time she didn't turn around. She got in her car and drove off.

"Nothing like leaving a man horny in the woods with a woody of his own," she mused.

Chapter 9
Damn, Freak is an Understatement

When Sinclair walked in the door, she saw she had four messages. This was unusual.

It can't be anybody but Aliette. She's got issues, but she couldn't possibly leave four messages. If it were that important, she would've called me on my cell phone.

She took off her shoes and listened to the messages. As she figured, the first two were from Aliette, and they both expressed how excited she was about the list she had to prepare. She also said she didn't want to leave it on the machine, so Sinclair should give her a call when she got in.

The third message was from Wayne. "Sin, what up? Call me when you get a chance. One."

The last was from Ja'qazz. "Sinclair, hello. I just wanted to say that I really enjoyed the time we spent together this afternoon. I'd like to talk about seeing you again. When you get a chance, give me a call at the club. Later."

She had to admit it was nice chilling in the park and making small talk with Ja. What made it even better was the fact that Aliette had no idea they had run into each other and that Sinclair now knew Ja was interested in her.

Man, I can't believe how this is all playing out, she thought as she got undressed. *I'll get relaxed then I'll call Aliette. I'm anxious to see what mess she wants to do for her bachelorette party. Can't imagine it will be too outrageous, but then you never know. Wonder what Wayne is gonna do for his bachelor party.*

She poured a glass of wine and picked up the phone to call Aliette.

"Yo."

"Hey, girl, what's happening? How was your day?"

"It was okay until just a few minutes ago. Wayne blew me off in a major way. I was out all morning taking pictures, and he worked on a project most of the day. I called him and asked if he could meet me for lunch and he said no. I was okay with that, but when I got home, his ass was out the door not less than five minutes later. I asked him where he was going and all he said was 'Out.' That was two hours ago. I ain't heard from him since."

"Well, maybe he's just hanging out, celebrating. I'm sure it's nothing more than that. Relax. You're so dramatic."

"Maybe you're right, but he's been acting a little bit weird lately. Do you think he knows about Ja'qazz and me? He may be getting last- minute jitters. You think? All I know is that I wanted to spend some time with him since I was hanging out this weekend, and he is totally not interested. I don't appreciate that."

"Are you feeling a bit guilty and as a result you think he's doing dirt?"

"Girl, please. Hell no. If he were taking care of the kitty, there would be no reason for me to be dreaming of getting it licked elsewhere. That's another thing. We haven't had sex in a few days.

That's a long time for us. I'm gonna need a dust buster."

"You buggin'. Maybe you got last-minute jitters. Don't worry. It happens to the best of us. So on to more exciting things. What are your fantasies, your secret want-to-but-don't-dare-to-do?

"Oh yeah. I was so excited when you left me that message. Let's see. I want another threesome, and this time I'm gonna take it in the butt, and I want to get real high and dance on somebody's table."

Silence came over the conversation.

"Hello? You there?" Aliette shouted.

"Yeah, I just can't believe you're down for that stuff. I know it's been a while since you last got your head tight so I can see that, but I never knew you had a threesome before. What was that about?"

Sinclair knew she had widened a wound that was not totally closed yet, but she had to do this to really know how to get Aliette. Hearing it from her would help put closure to the situation, allow her to know how Aliette felt about it while she was doing it, after it, and how it affected her life. The anxiety was eating her up, but she had to do it.

"No. I don't want to talk about it. It's the past, and I don't remember a lot of if anyway."

"Oh, I see how you do me. I thought we were girls. Your secret is safe with me."

"Alright, here it goes . . . I used to work part time for a small newspaper. They had writers of all kinds who would come up in there and do articles for them. There was this guy named Vernon who would come in and bring all of the ladies bagels and coffee almost every day. He was friends with one of the big-wigs. You know, I thought he was hot, but he was married, so the little flirting was never taken seriously by any of us.

"Until one day, he came in and you could see he was in rare form. Normally he would wear a sports jacket with a pair of khakis, chillin'. This time he wore a muscle T-shirt and a pair of jeans. He was wearing that shit, girl. Anyway, a few of us was like, damn bro, to what do we owe the pleasure of you coming in here pumping up our hormones?

"Then one girl—I forgot her name—pushed up. Bold as hell, she told him that a different time and a different place, she would take him. He sort of said, 'yeah, right.' They went back and forth while the rest of us drooled, then a proposition came up. She said she and any one of us would run a train on him and dared him."

Sinclair's heart was beating a mile a minute as she imagined Vernon flirting with this woman and loving every minute of it. She couldn't believe it still hurt so much after all this time, but it did. Aliette's story still didn't tell Sinclair everything she wanted to know, though.

"So are you saying you ended up being the third person?" she asked Aliette.

"Yeah. It took him a few days of this girl flirting with him for this guy to agree, but he did. She didn't really think he would, so she hadn't thought about who the third person would be."

"So you stepped up to the plate, huh?" Sinclair felt sick to her stomach as she asked.

"Girl, this brotha was fine. I wasn't about to pass up an opportunity like that. Besides, after hearing them two talk shit for so many days, I had to know if the man really had all those skills he kept bragging about."

Sinclair, of course, knew exactly what kind of skills Vernon had. Even though she wasn't into anything freaky with him, she'd always thought he was a great lover. As much as he had hurt her, it still pissed her off to hear Aliette talking about him like a damn piece of meat.

"So was he all that?" Sinclair asked.

"The first time was cool. Everybody was comfortable with each other and satisfied when all was said and done."

"Did you say the first time? Damn. How many times did y'all freaks do your thing?"

"It wasn't all that long," Aliette answered. "The next week he came in and we started talking shit again. We hooked up again, but this time it was at his house."

Sinclair felt a pain like a knife in her heart. They had been in her bed.

"We did it at his place for a while until the other chick suggested a change of scenery. She was a real gold-digger, so she suggested this real expensive hotel. I think she just wanted to see if he had the loot to pay for a room. So anyway, me and the girl are sitting there waiting when he walks in the room with this look on his face."

"What look?"

"Like someone had died or something. It turns out he has these pictures to show us. He said his wife had found out about our triangle and the shit hit the fan. Told us we were through. It was no big deal to me, ya know? I mean, I was just havin' some fun while it lasted.

"But a few days later, some pictures were delivered to my house too. Well, my husband at the time was very upset. We broke up and he moved in with one of his friends. He tried to fuck with me when we didn't really have anything for him to take. I guess his ego was bruised."

"That's how your marriage ended?"

"Yeah." Aliette didn't even sound upset. "The other girl was married too. She got the pictures and her husband basically did what mine did—divorced her and took everything. She did a'ight, though. I think she's a big-time editor at the newspaper now."

"So did you ever see the guy again?" Even though she was basically through with Vernon as soon as she saw the pictures, Sinclair still wanted to know if he had tried to hook up with Aliette again. This would have told Sinclair that for Vernon it was about more than the sex. She was glad to hear Aliette's answer.

"We didn't hook up anymore. He was totally distraught because his wife divorced him too. I believe he moved back to his hometown, somewhere in West Virginia. Never heard from him again."

"Damn, Al, you don't even sound like you give a shit. Didn't it upset you at all to get a divorce or to know you ruined someone else's marriage?" This was the whole point for Sinclair. It might have helped her heal if she knew Aliette at least felt bad, but that wasn't gonna happen.

"Shoot, I really didn't care, 'cause I ain't know his wife. Besides, I was having problems with my own damn marriage. We were only together for a few months and I lost interest in him. Getting married was a mistake for me back then because I wasn't finished doing my thing. Part of me still isn't."

"No kidding," Sinclair agreed.

"Hush. I got a really big sexual appetite. Besides the fact that I'm a huge flirt, I like to be looked at as sexy, and I want men to want me all the time, even if they can't have me. As foul as it sounds, it got me out of my marriage. I didn't fight him for anything. I just bowed out gracefully."

"So why didn't you tell me you were married before I pulled your card at Barry's?"

"I never mentioned it because it was so brief. We both got our own lawyers and handled it pretty painlessly. He tried to drag it out because he claimed it was my fault. He was a nice guy, but not in tune with his sexuality, not to mention mine. He was always scared to try new things. I used to like to go to go-go bars because they would get me hot and horny, and he was grossed out by me getting lap dances.

"One time, we were out and they had a contest. Whoever got up on the stage and danced would get fifty dollars. Naturally, after a few drinks I was up there, shaking all of my thangs. He got so angry—or embarrassed, I'm not sure which one—and grabbed me off the stage, making me fall and sprain my ankle. From that point, I knew it was just a matter of time. I was too wild for him. And so when he received those pictures, I was caught and it was fine with me."

Listen to her. She really couldn't care less about how she hurts people. Stank ho! She deserved that ass whipping that I dreamed about, Sinclair thought. When she spoke, though, she tried to keep the tone light. She wasn't ready to reveal her true feelings to Aliette until she'd gotten her revenge.

"So, you want a threesome, wanna get your ass plugged and you want to dance for someone. Is there anyone in particular you would like to dance for? Oh, and you wanna smoke some weed."

"Funny you should say that. When I first met Ja'qazz, I thought maybe I could have it with him. But I think I want him all to myself," Aliette said.

"You still need a third person in order to have a threesome."

"True, and this is where you would come in."

"Who, me?"

"Yeah."

"Girl, you tripping. I'm not sleeping with you and no other guy."

"Who said it had to be a guy? I already did that, remember? I was thinking more like me, you and another woman. Don't you know how sensual that is? Women know every part of another woman's body and that's what makes it out of this fucking world."

"You are a total freak, you know that?" Sinclair tried to sound like it was a joke.

"Don't hate, participate," Aliette answered. "I'm in tune with what needs to be done to Ms. Kitty Kat. If I don't make it happen, who will?"

"I tell you, you are too much for me. But, okay, we can manage something like that. There are plenty of people out there who are looking for the same thing you are."

Sinclair had no intention of sleeping with Aliette's freaky ass, but she was playing along until she could figure out her whole plan. For now, she turned the conversation in a different direction before Aliette could start going into any detail about the lesbian fantasy she had in mind.

"Aliette, let me ask you something. Are you sure you want to get married? Because whatever it is you're dreaming of about Ja has got you really bugging. An emotional affair is just as bad as the actual act of having sex. If you aren't careful, you may end up acting on those fantasies and not only would that not be good, he may start to develop feelings. What are you going to do then?"

"First of all, Ja'qazz is the typical man. He won't develop feelings. He'll just enjoy the ride. And secondly, I'm not married yet. I just want to freak one more time and get the shit out of my system."

"It's cool. We'll work it out. I'm going to bed. Catch up with you later."

Sinclair climbed into bed and thought about the conversation she'd just had. Revenge was going to be easier than she thought, as long as she could find a way to do it without actually having to sleep with Aliette and another woman.

As she lay in bed, Sinclair thought about what Aliette had said about the threesome with Vernon. While she wanted to cry, she had made herself a promise that the last time she cried would be just that—the last time. She would no longer allow this to rent space in her head and rip her apart inside. Granted, her pain would be a motivating factor in getting Aliette back, but she was handling it. She was okay for the moment.

Aliette's story had at least given her a little peace. Now she knew there wasn't any emotional connection between Vernon and the two women. His betrayal still hurt, but at least he had been truthful when he told her it was only about sex. If Aliette was telling the truth, he hadn't tried to contact either woman after Sinclair found out about them. Even if he had ruined their marriage, Sinclair could at least believe now he'd learned his lesson and felt bad for what he'd done.

The next morning, Sinclair went into the closet of her bedroom where she had tucked the pictures of Vernon, Aliette and the other woman; wrapped them so that they wouldn't get damaged; and packed them away for what she hoped was the last time. Then she made coffee, took a shower and went to work. When she got into the office there was a message from Ja on her desk and he left a number. After she got settled, she called.

"Hello. Can I speak to Ja'qazz?"

"This is Ja. Sin, is this you?"

"S'up? How you recognize my voice?"

"Man, your voice is all I hear. But before we go any further, do you have a few minutes?"

"Yeah. What's up?"

"I wanted to bring up something that we talked about yesterday. I feel funny about this thing with Aliette. I mean, she has you thinking I led her on, and I didn't. I really just want you to know I didn't make the move on her. I hope you believe me."

"Ja'qazz, I know the deal. Aliette lies a lot. It's all good."

"So you're not angry with me?"

"No. What is there to be angry with you about? You met me when the time was right for both of us, not just you. She, for whatever reason — well, never mind."

"I feel really relieved. You know you seem really special. The first time you came into the club you were really standoffish. All bougie and shit. I tried to make eye contact with you but you were in your own little world. Aliette did most of the talking, and when you walked away, I just knew it was gonna be difficult getting to you. I mean, I'm a confident guy, but I was really intimidated by you that night. Didn't you see me staring at you when you were at the door paying?"

"You know what? I did feel someone looking at me, but I didn't look around to see who it was. I didn't want it to be obvious I was uneasy. I brushed the feeling off. That was you? Why didn't you say something to me then?"

"Because you were with your girl, and like I said, I didn't know how to approach you. When you came back the second night, your girl was all up in my face. I paid for the drinks and she, not you, came up to me and talked. I guess that little mental moment between her and herself made her forget I needed to ask her something. I'm to blame, too, but none of that matters. When she was at the club the other afternoon, I finally got the opportunity to ask her to hook us up and to get me your phone number. She kind of laughed and completely ignored the question, so I gave up, but when I saw you at the fitness store and *you* approached *me*, I refused to let you go without getting into your head a little. I wanted you."

There was a pause then Sinclair's other line rang.

"Ja, I gotta go. I'll call you later, okay?" She really didn't want to stop talking to him but she had to take the business call.

"Yeah, that's cool. Later, baby."

She hung up with a smile on her face.

Chapter 10
Lies, Lies and More Lies

"Yes, Sinclair speaking."

"Sin, it's Aliette. Don't you know that this motherfucker didn't come home until five o'clock this morning? I paged him after we got off the phone. He didn't call me back for an hour, and when I asked him when he was coming home, he said he was out with the guys having a few drinks and he would be home soon. This was about nine o'clock."

"Okay, we talked about that. Why are you tripping? Where is he now?"

"In the other room. What? Why am I tripping? He been acting really fucked up, and it bothers me. But you know what? I'm just gonna chill. Leave it alone. We're getting married soon, and he's just cleansing his system of the shit. That's all. What did you do last night after we got off the phone?"

"Nothing. I just went to bed. I was tired. I thought about what you said, and I'm not down with that."

"What?" Aliette sounded disappointed. "It's a'ight. I can cut up by myself."

"I can cut up a little bit, but I don't smoke and I definitely don't do women. What are you doing around noon? Want to meet me for lunch?"

"Sure. Where, Barry's?"

"No. A nice and relaxing place. How about The Butta Cup on Adelphi?"

"I'll pick you up. See you then."

When Aliette hung up the phone, she couldn't help but question Wayne some more. He was in his office so she knocked and went in. He looked a hot mess, like he'd had too much to drink. The big drinker he wasn't, he had probably passed out somewhere and couldn't drive home. But there was a look about him going on. His body was there, but his mind was somewhere else.

"Hello, did you forget where you lived or even that you have a phone?"

"Please don't talk so loud, and no to both of your questions. Why you yelling? I called you and told you I would be home shortly. The shortly was just longer than I expected. I was chillin' with the guys, shooting the shit. Chill, it's not that serious."

"Not serious? You could have been lying dead somewhere and I wouldn't have even known."

"I don't know who you think you're fooling. You know gotdamn well that's not your concern. Knowing you, you probably thought I was out with some other woman. Breathe easy, girlfriend."

Something was definitely up. Aliette walked over to Wayne and looked him straight in the eyes.

"Is there something going on with you? You've been acting really strange this last week. You know we're getting married in a little over two weeks, right? Have the plans changed and I don't know about it? Are you nervous? Talk to me."

"Nah. I'm just chilling, enjoying my last days as a single man." He grabbed her and set her down on his lap. He looked Aliette in her eyes and thought *I can't marry her*.

"You know I love you, girl. I'm just hanging. Did you and Sinclair go and get her dress yet?"

"No. Not yet. We know where we're going, and the boutique has the dress on hold. Any alterations are made in house within twenty-four hours, so I'm not worried. In fact, I need to go for one more fitting before I get my dress. I'm so excited."

"Good, baby. Now let me finish this up, and we'll go out to lunch and talk."

"Oh, I can't. I'm meeting Sinclair at The Butta Cup for lunch. You're welcome to come if you want."

"No, you go ahead. I'm gonna lie down. I can finish this up later. I need to catch up on some much-needed sleep." He walked out of the office and into the bedroom to lie down.

"See you later then," Aliette said even though he was already out of the room. She left his office and pulled the door behind her. It wasn't closed all the way, and she heard the phone ringing. She stopped to listen as the answering machine came on and recorded the caller's message.

"Wayne, it's me. Call me when you get a chance. Talk to you soon. Bye."

She was shocked because not only was it out of the ordinary for Wayne not to answer the phone, but a woman had left the message. Aliette didn't know whether to go back into the office. What would she find in there, anyway? She walked away, pacing in the hall for a minute before she decided to go back and replay the message to see if she recognized the voice. When she went into the office, she noticed the message indicator light wasn't blinking. Wayne must have picked up the phone just as the answering machine came on and listened while the person was leaving the message. This would have automatically turned off the recording function so the message didn't register. She went into the bedroom only to find him stretched out across the bed.

"Wayne." He didn't answer

Dang, Sinclair! Wayne heard her, but he pretended to be asleep.

Alright, that's not cool. Who the hell was that on the phone? Aliette wondered. Immediately she went to look at the caller ID and the number was blocked.

"Damn it," she whispered. "Don't trip, just chill." She went ahead and took her shower and got ready for lunch with Sinclair. She refused to mess up her mood, so she put on something really chic and did her hair. Her makeup was tight, and she was ready to go. On her way out the door the phone rang again. She immediately ran to pick it up. When she answered, the person on the other end hung up.

Sinclair wasn't expecting Aliette to pick up the phone, so she hung up. She'd call Wayne back when she knew Aliette wasn't there.

"Whatever," Aliette said as she ran out the door.

Aliette was waiting outside Sinclair's job for her when a car pulled up in front of her. It was Ja'qazz. He got out of the car and went inside. Aliette watched him as he entered Sinclair's office, which was in the front of the building. Aliette could see right into the office through a large window. Sinclair's back was to the window when Ja walked in, so she hadn't noticed Aliette outside in her car. Ja made himself comfortable in a chair, and Aliette was able to see them talking like old friends. Wondering what he was doing there, she got out of her car and went in. As she came near the office, she heard them laughing and carrying on. Sinclair looked up in surprise as Aliette entered.

"What are you doing here so early?" Sinclair asked.

"Did you forget we had lunch plans?"

Sinclair had to think of something quick to explain why Ja was in her office. He had stopped by to ask her to go to the park with him during lunch hour, but she didn't think Aliette would want to hear that.

"No. I didn't forget. I was just finishing up with Ja'qazz. We're going to print a few fliers for him — or should I say for Barry's."

Sinclair looked at Ja as if to say *follow my lead*. She wasn't totally lying, anyway. A few days before, Ja had come into the shop and asked Sinclair about getting some fliers done for Barry's. She didn't usually handle accounts, but she had worked with Ja to design something then submitted the proposal to her boss, who would finalize the deal.

"Right." Ja went along with Sinclair's little white lie. "Get back to me on the cost so I can get a check cut. Aliette, how have you been? Long time no see."

"I've been laying low, and yourself?"

"Good. Just working. You know how that is. See you ladies later." He left in a hurry.

"Bye to you, too! I swear men get their periods too," Aliette complained.

There was obviously a bit of curiosity on Aliette's part about why he was there in Sinclair's office when Aliette knew full well Sinclair didn't handle printing contracts. She would be sure to mention this over lunch.

Go ahead and ask me why he's here. I dare you! Sinclair thought

"You ready? I'm hungry."

"Uh-huh, let's go," Aliette grunted.

As they drove, Sinclair could tell there was something up with Aliette, and Aliette could tell Sinclair noticed she was annoyed. If she asked her what was wrong, she would tell her about Wayne and what went on that morning. Aliette had to admit it bothered her more than seeing Ja in Sinclair's office.

The lounge wasn't too crowded and they were seated immediately. They both ordered Kendall Jackson Chardonnay and sipped while they browsed the menu.

Sinclair decided on a Chicken Caesar salad and Aliette ordered the same but with shrimp. When the waiter came back, they placed their orders. Once he was gone, Aliette took a deep breath and started to talk.

"You know, something really weird happened this morning. When I got off the phone with you, I went in and talked to Wayne. I told him I wasn't feeling him not coming home when he said he

would. He told me he was just chilling with the
guys and basically got caught up in the moment of
celebrating his last days as a single man. That's
cool, but when I was leaving his office, the phone
rang and he didn't answer it.

"Who was it?"

"I don't know. It was a woman's voice, and it
sounded like it was muffled. After a while I thought
I was gonna go back in and listen to it again, but
when I came back there was no message recorded. I
went in the bedroom to ask him who it was, but he
was sleeping. Then I went to the caller ID box and
the number was blocked. On my way out the door,
the phone rang again and when I answered it, I got
a big old click in my ear."

*That was me, dummy. I was about to tell Wayne
that you're a ho and he shouldn't marry your ass!*

"You don't think that's funny? I mean, lately
he's been strange. I'm trying not to read too much
into this shit but I'm telling you, he gonna make me
act up. Help, girl. What do you think is going on?"

"Personally, I think he's just nervous. He's
probably doing things he wouldn't normally do
because he's getting married and feeling a little bit
guilty, but not enough to talk to you about it. After
all, soon you will be Mr. and Mrs. Wayne Grieg. I
don't know. I wouldn't worry about it. I mean,
aren't you getting your last taste of things before
you jump the broom?"

"Yeah, but—"

"But nothing. What makes you think he's any
different? Men are all the same, and getting married
gives him more reason to cut up. So you can do one
of two things: You can trip over every move he

makes, or you can get over it. The choice is yours.
I'm tired of hearing about it."

"That's a friendly thing to say," Aliette
snapped, "but you're right. Maybe my guilty
conscience is eating at me a little bit, but then I
should be knocking it down with Ja as much as I
can since Wayne's out there doing his thing or
getting his thing done. Whatever!"

"Maybe you should," Sinclair responded as
she wiped her mouth.

As they ate their lunch, Sinclair was thinking
about the kiss she and Ja'qazz shared. It was
sensual, and the reality was whatever Aliette
dreamed happened between her and Ja'qazz didn't
matter. Sinclair had dated a little bit since
divorcing her husband, but not one of her dates
made her feel like Ja did. All tingly inside, she let
out a little sigh. Aliette looked up at her, but
Sinclair refused to return the stare and submitted to
the idea that she was going to take this Ja thing and
run with it.

*Why shouldn't I? I'm single and horny as hell.
She doesn't have to know — at least not now. She'll find
out when all is said and done, what goes around comes
around.*

Lunchtime was over and Sinclair had to get
back to the office. Buzzing as they often were, they
paid the bill and took their time walking out the
door.

"Thanks for coming out to lunch. I had a
relaxing time, and I'm stuffed and feeling lovely,"
Aliette said.

"Lucky you. You get to go home. I have to go
back to the office. It shouldn't be that busy. I just

have to look over the fliers Ja'qazz wants done then I'll be leaving shortly after that."

"Ah, how does Ja'qazz know where you work?"

Okay, here we go. Keep track of the lies so you don't get tripped up later, Sinclair thought.

"Well, I ran into him one day when I was out during lunch and he asked if I knew where he could get some fliers printed for a party that was going to be happening at Barry's. I told him I worked at a printing shop and that I could probably push it through as a priority. He stopped by and gave me the details."

"I didn't know you guys had even formally met."

"We hadn't, Al, since some rude person I know never bothered to introduce me to the man."

"Whatever, Sin." Aliette rolled her eyes.

"I introduced myself to him. Is there something wrong with that?"

Aliette didn't answer.

"Can I finish my story, or are you going to stay stuck on stupid and trip because he was in my office?"

"Go ahead," Aliette said as she sighed and looked the opposite way.

Ha! Ha! Ha! Is someone getting angry? Sinclair said to herself.

"His idea of graphics was a man and a woman wearing a tie-dyed tee with ripped jeans and bare feet. I laughed and told him that's what I wear on my days off. You know, he really seems like a nice guy. I'm surprised he doesn't have a girlfriend."

"How do you know?" Aliette growled.

"I don't know. He doesn't seem, let's see, attached, or interested in you, if you want my honest opinion."

"I didn't ask for your opinion, Sinclair," Aliette snapped

"Why couldn't I have been lucky enough for him to be interested in me or see me first?" Sinclair teased, knowing Aliette would never admit Ja had wanted to meet her from the start.

"Guess you're not that lucky." Aliette smiled smugly.

"Well, I think if the right woman came along, he would settle down. When are you planning to tell him about Wayne? Have you even thought about it? You know this can't go on for too much longer."

"Yeah, I know. And to be perfectly honest, I'm bored with him. He's acting like he's scared to hit it."

"How do you know he wants to hit it?"

"Who wouldn't want to get with me?" Aliette asked Sinclair as she put her hand on her hip. "I could go right now and get any man I want."

"Then I suggest you go and get Wayne because I really don't think Ja is feeling you, doll."

They stood there staring at each other. Sinclair was thinking maybe Aliette was the one with cold feet. To give up her stank ways didn't seem possible, even for the man who had been there for her through thick and thin.

"You need to go home and relax," Sinclair suggested.

"Whatever. Are we going out tonight?"

Sinclair didn't know if she was in the mood for any more of Aliette's drama that night, but she agreed anyway. She could always call later to cancel. "Yeah, we can do that if you want."

Aliette dropped Sinclair off at the office and she went home. When Sinclair got into her office, there was a note for her. It read:

Sinclair,

> *I see you put in for this job for Barry's Place. This could be big for the company. Glad to see you're working on getting new accounts. Good job!*

It was from Jeremy, the president of the company. Behind the note was a check for twenty percent of the cost of the job.

Oh, yeah, she thought. *This will definitely come in handy.* She sat down in her chair and swung around with a smile on her face. She decided she would go shopping right after work and pick up something sexy to wear and some new perfume. She was gonna look good tonight.

Paperwork was all over her desk. Even though she was getting tired from the two glasses of wine she had, the work needed to be done. As Sinclair diligently formatted an ad, she thought about Ja'qazz. How lovely it would be for them to hook up on the serious tip. She would treat him like the king he was, loving him every minute of the day and standing by his side when he needed her. Even children would be an option, as well as a house, a few dogs and a life that was normal. Feeling she had already fallen for him, at least on the physical level, she wanted to get to know him more on the emotional level. She wanted nights where they would just lay and cuddle and talk about anything that came to mind. They would take bubble baths with candles that dimly lit the room, and she would kiss his lips and taste his sweetness on hers.

It started to pour outside, and the sound of it dropping against her window was very peaceful. Sinclair knew for sure she wasn't going out. One more ad and she would call it a day — a very long day, so it seemed. As she turned around to shut off her computer and close her blinds, she looked out the window. The rain was coming down harder and harder by the minute.

"Great. It would be on the day I decided to do my hair."

Sinclair was still looking outside when she saw a figure approach the building and stand outside her window. It was a man with bags in his hands. He looked like he was delivering some food. She damn sure hadn't ordered anything.

"Who could it be, standing in the rain like a jackass?"

She planted her face against the window and covered the sides of her eyes so the light wouldn't hinder her sight. She looked harder and saw it was Ja'qazz. She was so surprised she just stared for a few moments more before she smiled at him. He came into her office dripping wet. He shook the rain off his DKNY jacket. In his hands were bags of food from the bistro on the pier. He set them on her desk then took off his coat.

"Let me take that for you," she said as she reached for his coat and hung it on the hook behind her door. *Damn, he is so fucking fine*, she thought. "What are you doing here?"

"I wanted to surprise you with dinner because this afternoon I missed out on lunch. I was disappointed, but promised not to let you get away from me tonight. When it started to rain, instead of asking you out I figured I would bring dinner to you. You're worth running out in the rain, don't you think?"

"Thank you. I was just saying to myself that I didn't feel like going out. Aliette and I were supposed to go out for a few, but then after two glasses of wine and all of this paperwork, I got tired as hell."

"Oh, and here — Kendall Jackson. I know it's your favorite. Well, Aliette said you guys drink Kendall when you do drink wine."

He placed a huge bottle of wine on her desk along with two glasses. Then he pulled a tablecloth out of the bag, pushed away some of the clutter on her desk and laid out the spread: chicken in a white wine sauce with mushrooms, asparagus, and almond rice accompanied by grapes, cheese and melons for dessert. She felt overwhelmed by romance and passion. The tingly feeling was all over, not just her spot. *He could get it for sure now*, Sinclair thought.

As they sat and chatted, Sinclair's cell phone rang several times. She was having the most romantic moment in her life so she totally ignored it. After it rang a few more times, she turned it off. Dinner was very nice. She turned the lights off so that only the reflection of the streetlights coming through the window would illuminate the room.

With the rain coming down and their silhouettes casting shadows in the window, the only thing missing was music. Sinclair excused herself and went into the main computer room. By then everybody had gone home, so she changed the station from elevator music to a station that fit the mood. When she came back into the office, Ja'qazz was standing there with the glasses in his hands.

"I want to propose a toast. To a friendship meant to be and a relationship that is hopefully in the making."

A kiss consummated their dinner. For Sinclair, the beginnings of a kiss told how it would end. As she took his tongue, his hands rose along her thighs. Caressing her hips and up to the small of her back, he touched her with great delicacy. He took her face in his hands and their passion grew. Not wanting this to be the place where they made love for the first time, Sinclair pulled away.

"What's wrong?"

"Nothing. Why don't we finish eating and go to my place? I think we'll be more comfortable there."

In agreement but still not able to keep their hands off each other, they began to pack up the food. When they were finished, Sinclair turned off the radio, straightened up her desk and went to draw the blinds, only to find Aliette standing right outside her window. Aliette had driven to her office after she couldn't reach Sinclair on her cell or home phones.

Their eyes met. Sinclair's mouth opened slowly as if she were about to speak, while Aliette's thoughts became that of a rabid dog, unfocused and full of rage. Aliette bit her bottom lip and panted as Sinclair proceeded to close the blinds.

Chapter 11
Caught Off Guard

Alliette couldn't believe what she had just seen. There was Sinclair chillin' with Ja'qazz, her sidekick — you know, her thing on the side. Her milkman, damn it! She turned around and walked to her car.

How could Sinclair do this, knowing what the deal was with her and Ja? Aliette couldn't wait until Sinclair called. Sinclair was always the one to try to make up when they had arguments or disagreements, and when Sinclair did call, Aliette was going to let her have it.

The nerve she has trying to rain on my shit. Jealous bitch. Just because she don't have no man and I have two, she want to play me out like that. That's cool. Just wait until I talk to that bitch, she thought as she got back in her car. *I can't believe that motherfucka!* She started her car and sped off.

While she was driving she turned on her cell phone, expecting it to ring at any moment. Not one ring sounded. During the entire drive home, Sinclair hadn't called. Aliette was getting angrier and angrier. Her stomach was cramping with anxiety, and she was getting a headache. As she pulled up to her house she saw that Wayne was home. The one time when she wished he wasn't home, he was. She couldn't go into the house this pissed off without him noticing. She took several deep breaths, inserted her key into the door and went in the house. As hard as it was to smile, she did. While asking him how his afternoon was, she walked over to the answering machine to see if there were any messages. There weren't.

"Did Sin call?"

"No. Why? Didn't you guys have lunch today?"

"Yeah, we did. I picked her up and we went to The Butta Cup."

"So why are you asking me if she called when—"

"What the fuck is your problem, Wayne?"

"I think you're the one with the problem, Aliette."

"Whatever." Her anger had gotten the best of her.

"You know what, Aliette?" Wayne started to say but changed his thoughts midway. "Never mind. How was your lunch?"

"Fine, how was your nap?"

"Good."

"Care to join me?"

"Join you where?"

"In the shower," she said in a blah tone.

"No. I want to watch the game."

Figures, she thought. *God forbid he got in the shower with me. We might actually end up fucking. I'm tired of this shit, coming home and not getting any from my so-called husband-to-be. Something's up, and I'm gonna get to the bottom of the shit. If he's cheating on me, I will find out. If he isn't, then we need to have a heart-to-heart to figure out what the problem is. Normal couples don't go this long without having sex or showing some type of affection.*

As she went into the bedroom, she started to take her clothes off. When she threw her shirt on the floor, she noticed a piece of clothing bunched up at the end of the bed. She practically ran to the bed, then grabbed the article. Adrenaline was making her see red, but as she examined it, she realized it was her camisole. She must have left it on the bed earlier and forgotten it was there. Relieved but still very hyped, she threw it on the floor with her other clothing and ran her shower.

She liked the water very hot so she could stand there and let it run down her back. This seemed to ease the tension in her shoulders. She turned forward and let the water douse her face. She thought about seeing Ja in Sinclair's office, and it burned her ass that he was there. But did she really have the right to be upset? *Hell, yeah*, she thought. He was her toy, not Sinclair's. A ringing phone took her out of her daze. She washed and conditioned her hair. While the conditioner set, she washed up with her Dolce & Gabana shower gel then rinsed off. She could hear Wayne talking on the phone, and this prompted her to rush out of the shower, dry off and throw her robe on. Feet still wet, she tiptoed out of the bedroom and into the hall leading to the living room. She could hear him whispering. Unable to make out what he was saying, she moved closer.

"Okay, baby. *Mwah!*"

She heard this and her jaw dropped to the floor. Standing in the hall, she threw her hands up then folded them on her chest. She quietly walked back to the bedroom and closed the door. Pacing the floor, she now knew why he had been so distant. Now she knew he was cheating on her for real and it wasn't her imagination. *How could I be so blind?*

she wondered. He was doing just what she used to do and acting like she used to act when she was cheating on him, except she still had sex with him — well, sometimes.

"Who the hell could it be?" she wondered out loud.

She rubbed her temples while biting her lip and decided to confront him. It had gone on long enough, whatever it was, and tonight was the night it was going to be over. She threw on her sweats.

"Fuck Sinclair. She can go to hell." Aliette wondered if she should call to cancel their plans for the night, or just not show up.

"She can go out by herself. I got my own shit going on."

She slid on her sneakers and stormed down the hall as she started to question Wayne. When she received no answer, she realized he wasn't there. She looked in the kitchen and his office, then heard a car running outside. Aliette went to the window and saw Wayne getting in a car that immediately pulled off after he was in.

That rat bastard! Where the hell is he going and with who?

In a rush, she changed into a pair of jeans and a jean shirt, grabbed her bag and ran out the door.

He can't be too far, she thought. "I'ma find his ass tonight."

Sinclair opened her front door while Ja got the food out of the car. She sat down and put her face in her hands. She shook her head as she remembered the image of Aliette standing outside her office window. Looking up at Ja as he came through the door with the bags, she felt like shit. Why? She didn't know. It wasn't like he was Aliette's man. She had a man, a man who she would be marrying. Again, Sinclair thought it served Aliette right. She closed her eyes and thought about her mother and what she would be saying to her right now if she were there.

"Baby, things happen for a reason. There are some things that are beyond your control. And sometimes, you have to go outside your character and play the part that fits you at that time. Revenge is sweet, but even sweeter when served by the hands of another."

"Oh, Momma." Sinclair sighed.

"How long do you think she was there?" Ja asked as he put the food on the table.

"I don't know, and you know what? I don't really think I care. Part of me feels like this was how she was supposed to find out. But then part of me feels like maybe I should call her and explain."

"I guess you should if you think it will help," Ja said.

"But explain what? How can you explain two people caressing each other to someone who really has no clue? Shit, I didn't plan for her to see us together like that, especially since I tried to play down why you were there this afternoon. I go back and forth all the time with mess like this with Aliette."

"I don't get your relationship with her. It's like there's some ulterior motive figured somewhere in this equation, but I can't put my finger on it."

Sinclair chose to ignore Ja's comment. She was a little spooked by the fact that he could sense there was not something right about their friend-ship.

"How do we explain this to her?" she wondered aloud.

"Sinclair, maybe you don't really need to explain anything to her. She just really needs to get over it."

"I know, and I hear you, but it's the fact that she saw us. Now I have no choice but to be honest with her about this whole thing."

"What haven't you been honest about?"

"Nothing, but I've been hurt in the past by some shit similar to this. I know how she feels. It wasn't by a friend, but the hurt was the same. That's another story. Maybe I should call her."

"No. I don't think you should. It was obvious she was upset. Give her some time to calm down. Why don't you go and take a hot bath? I'll make you some tea. What movies do you have to watch?"

"I don't know. Look in the entertainment center in the den. There should be some new DVDs there. Would you mind adding a little VSOP to that hot tea? I really need to relax. My body is really tense, and my shoulders are actually burning."

"No problem," he answered. As he was searching for the movies, the telephone rang. He didn't know if Sinclair would want him answering her phone, so he let the answering machine pick it up. Whoever it was decided not to leave a message. The phone rang again, and this time the caller stayed on the phone long enough for a message to register, but still the caller said nothing.

Oh well, he thought. Maybe it was some kids playing or something. He chose *Soul Food* to watch.

He remembered when he had seen that movie a while back. He liked it because regardless of the drama that went on, the end was very positive and reminded him that family and friends meant everything.

He could hear the bath water running and saw the steam coming from beneath the bathroom door. Curiosity was killing him. He already knew Sinclair had a great personality and her heart was sincere, but he was dying to know what that ass looked like.

Ja'qazz walked cautiously toward the bathroom door. He slid up against the wall and found the door was cracked. He couldn't really see because of the steam in the room, so he carefully inched the door open a little bit more. There, he watched Sinclair take off her clothes slowly and deliberately, as if she knew someone was watching her. As her panties dropped to the floor, his eyes went from her feet to her ankles to her calves to the back of her thighs to her ass, which was cute as hell with its little dimples. His gaze continued up. Her back was toned but feminine. It, however, didn't look like it had been rubbed in a while. Her movements were stiff. As she pulled her hair up into a bun and stuck pins in it, she bent over to swish the bubble bath throughout the tub. She was so sexy. How could someone not want to be next to her, to smell her, to make love to her and make her feel like she was the shining star of his universe? He swore at that moment to make her just that. If they got together, she would know he was hers. As he pulled back, Ja'qazz couldn't help but notice his penis was more than hard. Try petrified.

He awkwardly walked back into the den, pushing his member to the side, then made a detour into the kitchen to make the tea. As Sinclair had requested, he added a shot of VSOP to it and a slice of lemon. He grabbed a beer and went back into the den where he waited for her.

Sinclair came out of the bathroom. He watched her go into the bedroom and noticed she didn't close the door behind her. Was she asking him to come into the bedroom? Debating this, he sat there taking a swig of his beer and tried to read between the lines. As bad as he wanted her, he didn't want to push himself onto her, nor did he want to make her feel he was all about the physical. There was no denying she turned him on, but he wanted Sinclair on her own terms. She didn't come out and say that she wanted to have sex. A little kiss and fondling didn't mean that. Yes, it meant they had chemistry and they found each other attractive, but sex was a totally different thing. That could change someone's feelings as soon as it happened, and he wanted to do this right.

Given everything that had happened over the last few days, he didn't want to be the reason why she was tense. In fact, he wanted to be the opposite. He wanted her to feel safe and uninhibited when she was around him. Still not knowing whether he should go in the bedroom, he just sat and waited for her to come out. A few minutes later, she came out in a cute little two-piece boxer set. Gray-and-black pinstripes fell on her slim body. She sat next to him, smelling of citrus.

"What did you pick for us to watch?"

"*Soul Food*. I really like that movie. How's that sound to you?"

"Good. Start it."

They watched the movie, laughing at some parts and becoming very serious during others. Ja was sitting in the corner of the sectional and she lay with her feet on his lap.

She'd just had a pedicure, so she felt confident she could handle any wisecracks he might try to make about her feet. But on the contrary, he took them in his hand and brought them up to his lips. He ran his tongue in and out of her toes as he softly caressed her calves. Easing off the couch, he knelt in front of her and continued to rub both of her legs, each time going higher and higher up her thighs. Sinclair felt like she was in heaven. She closed her eyes and let him rub her down. Then, he moved up to her hips, rubbing them in a circular motion. Wondering if he could feel the heat that was brewing between her legs, she swung one of them over his head and made sure he could. He slowly slid his fingers inside her. She couldn't help but let out a sigh that invited him to go deeper. The phone rang, but that didn't break into their moment. Ja pulled her shorts to one side and kissed her lips. He slipped his tongue inside of her, softly playing tug-of-war with her clit. She couldn't believe how wet she was and how far his tongue went in.

After Ja'qazz slid her shorts off completely, he removed her shirt. She was even more beautiful than he thought. Staring in her eyes, he stood, pulled off his shirt then took off his pants. The moment they both had been waiting for was about to happen.

Sinclair grabbed his hand and led him into the bedroom. As she walked past the phone on the table, she noticed the light was blinking. She ignored it, continuing to take him in the room and laying him on the bed. She pulled him out of his boxers and put her warm mouth on his penis. Licking his balls and pushing his legs up, she tasted him. He pulled her up onto him and sat her on his lap. The initial feeling was a burning one, but when she started riding him, her juices gave it more of a tight, warm sensation. She rode him while he gently sucked on her nipples. The heat created a scent that consisted of their sweat and her citrus splash. It was a musky scent.

She whispered in his ear. "What are we doing?"

"You have to ask?"

The motion of her hips intensified; she was about to explode. He took the opportunity to explode with her. As each of them let go, she could feel him pulsating inside of her. Grabbing his back and pulling him as close to her as possible, they submitted to each other. Moments went by before either of them moved. They wanted to hold on to the moment for as long as they could. Neither of them said a word.

Ja'qazz slowly took the pin out of her hair and clawed at her mane until it fell on her sweat-speckled shoulders. She leaned back from him but remained on his lap. A sweet kiss of satisfaction was exchanged then she got off him. Smiling, they walked back into the den, butt naked, and Sinclair took this opportunity to listen to the message. It was Aliette. They looked at each other as the message played.

In a low and very weak voice, Aliette had left this message:

"Sinclair, I have been trying to reach you for a few hours now. Your cell phone is off and you're not answering your home phone. I need to talk to you as soon as possible. Call me."

As disturbing as this message sounded, Sinclair didn't think now was the time for her to talk to Aliette. Not only did Sinclair not want to ruin the mood — hell, she just got sexed up after being celibate for months — but she knew from the sound of Aliette's voice that calling her back would only lead to an argument.

"Are you gonna call her back?" Ja asked.

"No. She can wait. Now's not a good time. Besides, it would ruin our thang we got going on," she said as she tickled his sexy, hairy stomach.

They wrestled onto the couch, rewound the movie to where they left off and she sipped her tea, which was now cold, while he finished his beer. Sinclair fell asleep almost immediately and Ja'qazz left shortly after that.

The next morning was a free one for Sinclair, so she decided she would go to see Aliette. Sinclair also decided to be totally honest with whatever Aliette threw her way. *I'ma tell that crazy heifer just what it is.*

Dressed really cute, Sinclair got in her car and started making her way over to Aliette's house. She couldn't help but smile as she thought about how her evening had been. One would think she would be sore after all that action, especially since she hadn't been sexually active. It must have been around three o'clock in the morning when Ja kissed her on the nose and left. She was too tired to get up from the couch and into her bed so she just stayed there, totally relaxed and tension free.

As she pulled up to Aliette's house, she saw both Wayne and Aliette were home. She rang the doorbell and went in. Wayne sat at the table typing on his laptop.

"Hey you, long time no see. What's happening?" Sinclair asked.

"Not a thing, girl. Just handling this paperwork. You know how it is. Keeping busy, for sure. You know I have a wedding to pay for."

"Do you really?"

He shook his head no.

"I hear ya, bro. Where she at? And ah, we need to talk."

"She's in the living room, mad as usual. Maybe you can talk to her because I'm tired of trying. And yeah, we need to exchange notes."

"Al, where are you?" Sin called out. She walked into the living room and found Aliette sitting on the couch, flipping the channels. "What's up, girl? I got your message this morning."

"You know what? First of all, I want to tell you that I think you're fucked up. You know gotdamn well I was hooking up with Ja'qazz and you trying to fuck him anyway. What happened to you last night? I thought we were going out."

"I know. We were but after—"

"After what? After you and Ja were slobbing each other down in your office it was too late?"

Wayne heard Sinclair and Aliette arguing and stopped what he was doing.

"Wait a minute. I'm really not sure who you think you talking to like that, but are you sure you want to have this conversation here? Because you know we can—"

As Aliette got up to close the French doors that lead into Wayne's office, she continued her rant. "I called your cell phone several times, and when your ass didn't answer, I thought I would come down to the office to see what was taking you so damn long, only to find you in his arms and him rubbing your ass. What the hell's going on?"

Wayne got up and stood outside the room with his ear against the door.

"Well, to be perfectly honest, the day I saw Ja in the sporting goods store and after formally introducing myself to him—because see, you have yet to do that—we took a ride to the park and vibed. It turned out he was trying to ask you to hook him up with me when you hit on him in the back room. Then when he mentioned to you a second time he was interested in me, you basically told him I was on a leave of absence on the dating scene. I understand you wanted to make your little dream of him come true, but guess what? It ain't gonna happen. As good as it was for you, it was just that: for you, in your selfish mind, and that was it. You and Ja never existed. You flaunted yourself around him anytime you could and even more at the mention of me. So when we saw each other that day, it was the beginning of a friendship. I didn't plan for it to go this way, and when I saw that it was, I was unsure for a little bit. But then I thought about it. Why should I not take it further when it was me who he was interested in from the beginning? You were just the vehicle he was trying to use to get to me, and when you said nothing to me about that and tried to take him for yourself, I figured I would do both of us a favor. For me, I'll see where this can go, and for you, I'll take him off your hands, because see, bitch, you're getting married, so your ass shouldn't be seeing him or nobody else for that matter. So before you start talking shit, know this: your man is in there typing on his laptop and my man is at work, getting ready for the afternoon crowd at Barry's Place. Okay? Heard me?"

"You got a lot of nerve. You know damn well I was feeling him and we were gonna hook up before I got married."

"You got issues and I refuse to sit here and explain myself to you about a seeing a man who isn't yours. I mean, damn, you fantasize about him and now he's yours? Come on, get real. You really need to get it together. Ja and I have enjoyed our relationship up until this point, and based on that, we plan to jump into it with two feet. You, at the very least, ought be happy for me, not giving me shit. I have dated off and on and have had nothing but losers blow up my cell phone. Now when someone comes along against your wishes because you wanted him for yourself, you're jealous. Green is not your color. Get over it and be my friend, if that's what you are, or else fuck you."

Aliette stood there with her hands on her hips, fuming. But what could she say? In essence, Sinclair was absolutely right.

"Yeah, alright. It's cool."

"Good. I'm glad. I would hate for this to come between us. You know what I'm saying? So what else is on your mind?"

Trying to separate the two issues, Aliette attempted to lower her voice and tell Sinclair about the previous night. But it was too late. Wayne had heard their whole conversation.

Fucking slut, he thought as he remained standing outside the doors and continued to listen.

"I was getting out of the shower and caught the tail end of a conversation Wayne was having. He said, 'Okay, baby. *Mwah.*' You know, the kiss sound. I didn't know what to do, so I threw some clothes on and went to confront him, but when I came out the bedroom, his ass was hopping in somebody's car and they were gone."

"Where'd he go so fast?"

"How the hell do I know? I grabbed my bag and went after him, but I couldn't find him. I have no idea who it was he was talking to or what kind of car he left in. I'm telling you, something's going on. I'm so sure, and I need to know before I marry him."

"And if it is, what do you think you're going to do about it?"

"I'm not marrying a cheating man!"

"You don't fucking get it, do you, Al?"

"I don't want to hear that shit right now, Sinclair. Are you going to listen to me or not?" Aliette yelled.

"Go ahead," Sinclair said as she tried to remain composed.

"While I was out, I tried to call you, but your cell phone was off and you didn't answer your home phone. I called twice before I left you that message. Then I was crying all crazy and shit. I sort of roamed the streets, hoping to see him in passing, but I didn't. So I just came back home, but he still wasn't here. He just got in."

"And?"

"Am I supposed to take his excuse that he was just getting this out of his system as his reason for staying out all hours of the night? Doesn't this seem a little wrong or suspicious to you?

"I don't know. I mean, guys normally do this sort of thing a week before or the weekend of the bachelor party. I have heard of that. But look at what we were just arguing about."

"What does that have to do with anything?"

"Maybe all this time you thought Wayne was forgiving you and taking you back, ole boy was doing his thing."

"He doesn't have the balls."

"I think he does, and honestly, Aliette, you get what you deserve."

"But I still fucked him when I was doing my thing most of the time. He barely touches me anymore."

"So you're a self-proclaimed ho. Yippie ya yay!"

"What, bitch?"

Sinclair laughed. "Oh, God. This is funny to me."

"Well, I'm glad you're finding my problem comical."

"You're right. You do have a problem. But this problem didn't just happen. It's been here. You were just too busy getting your last dick to see it. You've been fucking around on Wayne ever since we've met."

Aliette was shocked at Sinclair's remarks.

"Sin, do you know something I don't?"

"Nope. We know the same things," Sinclair answered as she got up, grabbed her purse and turned to leave. She opened the French doors to find Wayne listening intently. He stuck his head in the room.

"Where'd you learn to whisper, Aliette, in a helicopter?" He walked away and said to Sinclair, "Thanks for the notes."

Sinclair knew exactly what that meant. Aliette, on the other hand, was clueless, as usual.

Chapter 12
The Moment of Truth

Sunday morning, the birds were singing, and it looked like it was going to be a nice day. Wayne lay awake looking at Aliette while she was sleeping. He knew that she had suspicions about him but at this stage of the game, the only information he was hiding was that there wasn't going to be a wedding. Normally when someone stepped out on his or her mate, it was because there was something missing. He had thought their relationship was good, as far as he knew, but somewhere along the line they'd lost something — or maybe they'd never had it.

When they made love, the passion was meek and the act itself was quick. No talking and touching made it more like a chore than anything else. Then, for some reason, Aliette started nagging about everything. Nothing that he did was right. Nothing. If he cut the grass, she would complain about the blades that got on the sidewalk. If he cooked dinner and it wasn't ready at a certain time, she would decline to eat. If he fixed an appliance in the house, she would complain it wasn't done right regardless if it was up and running.

When they first met, she had a very different look about her. Some might say exotic, but he thought she had a different look about her now, almost used up. No situation was urgent, yet she had mad drama all the time. It was like they couldn't come to a happy medium about anything.

Now, she walked around frowning half the time and taking pictures of everything and anything. To come out and talk to her would only result in an argument because she was always so defensive.

During the course of their relationship and before he asked her to marry him, she had cheated on him. Once, Wayne was supposed to fly out to San Diego for the day and come back late that night. His flight was supposed to come in around 11:00 P.M. but got in two hours earlier. When he called for her to pick him up she didn't answer the phone so he had to take a cab. He had arrived home with flowers in his hand. He went into the house only to find her having sex with another man. Needless to say, he was upset, lost control and kicked the guy's ass. They argued, didn't talk for a few days, but since he was committed to her and he loved her, they worked through it.

It took months for Aliette to win back his trust. She apologized daily and appeared to have great remorse for putting their relationship in jeopardy and swore that it meant nothing and wouldn't happen again. But it did. Some of them Wayne knew about, others he didn't. And ever since, he found himself just going through the motions of their relationship. He wasn't there emotionally and as little as possible physically. But something in him loved her unconditionally and he couldn't cut the ties.

Lately, it had gotten worse, and the latest information that Sinclair had given him was the final straw. Now he was pretty certain Aliette was up to her old tricks, and he was feeling the need to just end things. Shortly he was supposed to be getting married, knowing full well she wasn't good to him or for him. Loving her was easy — she had a good heart — but in love, he was not. Seeing how she had been really riding his coattails, asking him where he'd been, and being visibly annoyed when he came in late, now was the time to tell her the truth about what he knew and how he felt.

Quietly getting out of bed, he tried not to wake her. He had to work up the nerve for what was about to happen. Breakfast was a good idea, so he started the coffee, made eggs, bacon, biscuits and grits. He thought he might be wearing this food rather than eating it when he dropped the bomb on her.

The phone rang. He answered it and heard Sinclair's voice.

"Hey Wayne, is Aliette up?"

"No. Actually, she's still sleeping. Sinclair, while I have you on the phone, she was trying to hook up with that guy, wasn't she?" There was a pause.

"Yes, Wayne, she was."

"I don't know why I ever thought she would change. How many have there been? How many other men has she been with that you're aware of?"

Ding! Ding! Ding! Ding! Ding! The bells went off in Sinclair's head. This was the chance she'd been waiting for.

"Too many, Wayne." There was silence on the other end.

"Go on, tell me," he finally said.

"Wayne, I wasn't there when she hooked up with these other men. I knew of Aliette before we met in the park that day, but not by my choice."

"What? What are you talking about?"

"One day, I received pictures in the mail of my husband, Vernon, Aliette and another woman fucking."

"You're not serious."

"As a fucking heart attack. So serious that the shit ended my marriage."

"Oh, my God. How long ago was this, Sinclair?"

"About a year ago, and she was seeing some dude named Donnie too. I don't know for how long, but I know for sure she was fucking him, and he was married."

"I can't even cry."

"Don't, bro. I know how you're feeling right now, and trust me, I've cried enough for the both of us."

"Why didn't you tell me?"

"Why would I, Wayne? Hell, I was still in my own hell, dealing with my desires to get revenge. That's how it started off. I wanted to get her back for coming into and ruining my life."

"Sinclair . . . you . . . I don't know what to say."

"There's nothing you can say, Wayne. Something about Aliette isn't allowing her to love herself, and that's why she can't truly love or be committed to anyone else."

"That makes sense, Sin. Look, I gotta go. I'm gonna talk to her this morning and let her know I just can't go through with marrying her."

"Keep your head up, Wayne. Things happen for a reason, and sometimes you have to go outside your character and play the part that fits you at that

time. Revenge is sweet, but even sweeter when
served by the hands of another. My momma used to
tell me that."

"Thanks, Sinclair."

"Bye, Wayne."

Shortly after Wayne hung up with Sinclair,
Aliette came out of the bedroom.

"Nice spread. What's the occasion?"

"No occasion. Want some coffee?"

"Sure. Who was that on the phone?"

"Wrong number. Did you sleep good? I was
watching you. Did you feel me looking at you?"

"No. I was knocked out."

"Al, I need to talk to you. I know you've been
noticing some changes in me lately, and quite
frankly, my feelings for you have changed."

"That's obvious."

Wayne ignored the way she rolled her eyes at
him and said, "First, you should know I think you
are truly a good person, and I love you very much.
The problem is I'm not in love with you anymore."

"Oh, really?" she said casually as she went to
get a mug and pour herself some coffee.

"Yes, Aliette, really."

"Wayne, let me ask you something. When did
your feelings change? I mean, we've been through a
lot of things. I've compromised our relationship
and you still took me back. Why now are you trying
to roll out?" She sounded like she didn't believe
this was serious.

"You know, Aliette, you ask that like it's
wrong to give people chances to get it right. I

thought sticking it out with you would make you a better person. I loved you."

She pulled the chair away from the table and sat down. A few moments passed before she responded.

"You haven't been paying me any attention for months now, Wayne. I should be the one bailing out of this relationship. Between you being stingy with the dick and the mysterious phone calls, shouldn't I be sitting you down and having a talk with you?"

"It's not always about you, Aliette."

"Well, it must've been, because you stayed with me."

"You are a self-centered bitch."

"That may be true, Wayne, but I gets mine."

"Yeah, and apparently everybody else's too."

"What the hell is that supposed to mean?"

"I heard every bit of that conversation—or should I say argument—that you had with Sinclair. We're getting married and you were trying to get one last fuck before we did. And you have the nerve to have an argument with Sinclair because he was hooking up with her and not you. You have issues that have nothing to do with anyone but you."

"Don't judge me. If you were taking care of business, there wouldn't be a need for a man to clean up behind you."

"What about a woman? Would there be a need for a woman? You have been down that road, haven't you?"

"Who told?" Aliette's face finally showed some emotion. She was shocked that he knew her secret.

"It doesn't matter! The fact is I've been venturing out and doing things that you were very unaware of. My lifestyle has become one that is different from yours, Aliette."

"Ha! What exactly have you been doing, Wayne? This is cute. Humor me, please," she said as she sat back, folded her arms across her chest and smirked at him.

"You have no soul, Aliette. We're not getting married. I'm not in love with you."

"I get that, Wayne, but you still haven't told me what you've been doing."

"Aliette, I'm going to be a father."

"What? What did you say?"

"I am going to be a father. I have a child on the way."

"You fucking asshole." She hurled the mug of coffee at him. It missed his head and shattered against the wall.

"That's right. You wanted to know, so here we go." Wayne was furious, more so at himself. He should have known after literally catching Aliette in the act the first time that she really didn't love him. He continued. "One night when I was out, I met a woman. We talked for a while and developed a friendship. We started meeting for lunch or having drinks. One thing led to another and we slept together. On numerous occasions."

"So I was right."

"That's not all. I also went out with my boys a few times, tied a few on, and there was a little bit of touching and feeling there as well. No, I haven't had sex with them, but I have desires that really don't coincide with yours, and I feel it's best to get this out now rather than later."

"Oh, now you slob the cob." Aliette was practically laughing.

"Are you listening to me?" Wayne yelled.

"All I know right now is that you're about to be a daddy and you suck dick."

"Honestly speaking, when you cheated on me the last time with that dude, that wasn't even it. It was the conversation I overheard. It told me that all your apologizing and remorse was just bullshit. You had every intention of continuing to sleep around before and after we got married."

"That's not true."

"The hell it ain't."

"You can believe whatever you want. I don't give a fuck."

"Aliette, you never did!"

"So what're you saying? You're leaving me for her?"

"Baby girl, look, there's someone out there who fits your definition of a man and has the patience and understanding you need. It ain't me. I guess I really needed to hear you talking to Sinclair about some guy you trying to fuck. That opened my eyes. It's never going to end with you. Think about it. Do you even want to get married? You got mad at Sinclair for hooking up with someone you planned to hook up with before we got married. What's up with that?"

"He pursued me, Wayne!"

"Sinclair has been there for you endless times, and you know what? You're gonna need her even more now 'cause I'm so out this piece, so you better make sure that guy doesn't come between you and her. Accept it the same way you have to accept what I'm telling you now."

Pausing, he looked at her and saw nothing. No emotion, no tears, no nothing.

"You're not going to say anything?"

"Talk about fucked up. I may have cheated, but I didn't get pregnant. Who is this woman? Do I know her?"

"Look at you. You need to be thinking about the shortcomings of our relationship but instead you're more concerned with who this woman is. Did you hear anything I said to you? My intention wasn't to argue with you because you had to see this coming. We barely talk, touch or do anything together. The young lady—no, you don't know her and you don't need to. And I don't need to disclose anything about her to you so you can harass her. No thanks. She's carrying my baby, and regardless of whether she and I end up together, I want her to have a healthy pregnancy so she can deliver a healthy baby. Trust me, if we were going to come to this point, I would do it differently, but this is what it is."

"You know what, Wayne? You can try to justify what you've done all you want. I got time invested in this relationship, not to mention money, and you just want me to walk away? I don't think so. Why can't we try counseling? Maybe we can try to focus on the things that have been bothering both of us and work on repairing our relationship."

"We're done. Sorry. I made plans to move out during the week. I remember you mentioning you wanted to go and enter a few of your pictures in an art exhibit. Do that. I was gonna take that opportunity to move my things out while you were gone. I figured it would be better if you weren't here. I won't be taking anything but my clothes. You can have the contents of the house."

"You got an apartment? How long you been planning this?" By this point she wanted to cry but refused to show any sign of weakness.

"That doesn't matter, and yes, I have my own place. But don't worry. I set aside six months of rent for you to draw off in a separate account. The accounts we have together, I've signed the proper paperwork to have my name taken off. The funds that are in there are for you as well.

"I'm going to do some errands. I'll probably be out all day, so I guess I'll catch you later." He walked away, leaving the breakfast he had made for them on the counter. He could feel the heat from her stare on his back though as he left the room.

The confrontation had gone very differently than he had expected. All he knew was that he was relieved he had finally gotten this off his chest. Deceiving her was making him sick, almost depressed, and it would have been worse for sure if she busted him, because then she would have taken that window of opportunity to act up for sure.

Fire was coming out of Aliette's ears. *Who the fuck does he think he is, cutting me off like that? Punk bitch can't handle a little turmoil As soon as something goes wrong, he wants to bail out. Okay. He can do that, but I ain't going out that easy. And as far as the bitch he got pregnant, I'll find her ass too.*

As she watched him leave, she wanted to knock the hell out of him. But no, she just sat there as tears finally welled in her eyes and ran down her cheeks. She wasn't going to give him the satisfaction of seeing her break down. She went back into the bedroom and closed the door.

Aliette couldn't believe what was happening to her. As she cried the phone rang. She looked at the caller ID and saw it was Sinclair. Aliette didn't want to let her know just yet what was going on, so she let the machine pick up. She wasn't ready to tell Sinclair Wayne had just walked out on her. Not only that, she now had to send out cancellation notices to the invited wedding guests. Not that there were many, maybe thirty, but just the thought of doing it made her cry even more.

Aliette hadn't spoken to her mother in a very long time, but she knew just what she would say if she knew about this latest mess. Aliette and her mother had never really been close. She always told Aliette it was going to take a certain type of man to be able to handle her and her selfish ways. Not everybody could deal with someone who constantly lies and deceives. Her mother had watched her go through this time and time again. Every one of Aliette's boyfriends had eventually left her when he could no longer deal with her selfishness, and each time Aliette would try to make the breakup look like his fault, not hers. But her mother knew Aliette was difficult. And now that it was happening again, her mother would be able to say, "I told you so."

Chapter 13
A Little Her-Story for Ya!

It was late evening, and after crying for hours and falling into a deep sleep, Aliette woke up with a headache. She could tell she had been gritting her teeth because her jaws were hurting. Reaching for the phone, she heard someone at the door. A nervous, crampy feeling came over her stomach. She set the receiver back down and went to see who it was. As she approached, Wayne was coming in. Lips tight and fists balled, she went after him. She punched, kicked and grabbed him, but she wasn't getting the feeling she was hurting him in any way. She pushed him back out the door and closed it in his face.

"This is not your house anymore, so don't fucking come here unannounced."

"What are you talking about? I told you I was coming back to get my stuff."

"Yeah, well, you need to make an appointment next time."

"Aliette!"

"Wayne, beat it or I'll call the cops." She was in her survival mode, the most destructive mode of all for her. When she was feeling this way, she became cold and callous and took on a whole new personality.

She reached into her purse and pulled out some Tylenol. It was 8:30 in the evening and she decided she would take a shower then go out to have a drink to think about how she was going to break the news to everybody. Sinclair would be easy. She wouldn't throw it up in her face. *But then again, the way she's been breaking on me lately, I don't know*, she thought. It was her family, to whom she almost never spoke, who she worried about calling.

Her family lived in Baltimore, Maryland, on Booth Street. Her mother, Grace, regardless of how Aliette tried to explain to her that she wasn't entirely to blame, would believe Aliette caused the breakup. Manny, Aliette's brother who was wheelchair bound ever since he was hit with a stray bullet, could go either way. There was a time in her life when Aliette felt like Manny had her back and would always support her, but things had changed, so he might be supportive, or he might say it was all her fault. Then there was her sister, Patrice, who attended a local community college for radio broadcasting and worked part time at a local radio station. Patrice had never lived with a man, let alone married one, so Aliette couldn't give a shit what Patrice thought, even though she was pretty sure Patrice would only have negative things to say.

Growing up, Aliette and Patrice weren't close at all. There was a three-year difference in age, Aliette being the eldest. Patrice was her mother's favorite. Anything she wanted, she got. When their mother went out to the store, Patrice was right there following along because she knew she would get something if she went with her. Aliette was so jealous of their bond.

As they grew older, the sisters became a little closer, but they still argued daily. If it wasn't because Aliette was wearing Patrice's clothes, it was because Patrice's side of the room was always messy. If it wasn't because Patrice was hogging the phone it was because Aliette was in the bathroom for hours on end. The list of arguments went on and on.

Once Manny and Aliette's relationship changed, it only made things worse between her and Patrice. Manny and Aliette were only a year apart in age, and they had hung together pretty tight when they were younger.

Manny was a great basketball player, but always seemed to be drawn to the wrong crowd. In high school, he had the misfortune of being in the wrong place at the wrong time. A gang fight was going down and while he was watching from the sidelines, he got shot. As a result he lost use of his legs.

From that point on, Manny changed. Wheelchair bound, he put all his energy into helping his little sister Patrice. He took all the money he got from hustling and helped put her through school. Anything she needed, if his mother couldn't buy, he bought. Needless to say, this ruined the close relationship between Manny and Aliette, who became bitter and jealous. She would hide Patrice's schoolbooks and supplies and purposely ruin her clothes.

When Patrice was in her mid-teens, she got a boyfriend. Now, everybody knows what the first love can do to you. Greg was everything a young girl would want. Captain of the football team, he was also an awesome basketball player and could sing like a bird. He was also two years older than Patrice, one year younger than Aliette. Fully aware her sister was in love with Greg, Aliette sent him love letters. In them, she described what she would do to him if he would only give her a chance. She insisted her little sister didn't know what to do with him, that he should want a woman, not a little girl. Greg had received about seven of these letters from Aliette but had never responded to her advances.

One day, when everybody was sitting on the porch, Greg told Aliette in front of everyone that he wasn't interested in her and would appreciate it if she would stop writing him letters. He handed all of the letters to Patrice and let her read them.

Her mother was more than angry and sent Aliette to her room while Patrice cried with embarrassment and bruised feelings. As Aliette went upstairs, she nearly tripped over her smile.

In her room, she lay across her bed, satisfied with what she had done. As she glanced across the room, she noticed the pillow on Patrice's bed was not straight. There was something under it. Aliette walked over to the bed and lifted the pillow to find Patrice's journal, probably the most private thing a teenage girl could have. *Whiney bitch*, she thought. *I can't stand her ass. She thinks she's so cute and better than everybody. I got a trick for her. The next time she gets in my face, she's gonna regret it.*

Aliette planned to read the journal to find some incriminating evidence she could use to finally ruin the perfect image everyone seemed to have of Patrice. She started to read and was so engrossed she didn't hear her mother opening the door. Still fired up from what had happened, her mother snatched the book from her. Aliette quickly stood as if she was ready to get down with her mother. In slow motion, or at least it seemed to Aliette, her mother drew back and slapped her in the face so hard she cut the inside of her cheek.

"I'm tired of you always trying to bring Patrice down. Why don't you try building yourself up instead?" her mother shouted.

"Why are you always taking her side?"

"Because you're a liar and you own ill will, Aliette!"

"Get out of my room!"

"Girl, don't make me go upside your head again. You just like your father," she said as she left Aliette's room and closed the door behind her.

"So what," Aliette yelled at her mother through the closed door. She was confined to her room for the rest of the summer, and from that point on she was labeled as the troublemaker of the family. She wore the title very well. But without Patrice's journal to use as ammunition, Aliette would have to come up with another way to get her family's attention.

Sitting in her room with nothing to do but think gave Aliette plenty of time to come up with a plan. She decided she no longer wanted to live with her mother, sister and brother. She called her father and told him what had happened. Of course in her version of events, she was the victim. Her father agreed to let her move in with him, but only on the condition that she would work after school and when she graduated, she would either go to college or join the military. Agreeing, she held on to this information until the right time, which would be during another argument with Patrice. Her brother was now a potential opponent, too, since he had almost totally dropped their relationship and indulged in Patrice.

Aliette ignored her mother's call for dinner because she was too busy roaming through Patrice's closet for something she could put on. Aliette knew this would upset Patrice and would ultimately start the argument she wanted. About a half-hour later, she came downstairs wearing Patrice's favorite jeans. Patrice glared at her. Normally, Patrice would just let her mother handle something like this. She only started arguments with Aliette when her mother wasn't around to take care of her. But this time, she was still upset about the letters and she'd had enough. Before Aliette knew it, Patrice jumped on top of her sister. Food was flying everywhere while their mother tried to break them apart.

With great force, Patrice pushed Aliette down to the floor and started punching her. Receiving every blow, Aliette was feeling around on the floor for anything that would get her sister off her. She got a handle on something, and although she was unsure what it was, she held it tight and swung at Patrice. Until she saw the blood all over her clothes, she didn't realize she had grabbed a knife and sliced her sister right across her face. Aliette froze as she saw Patrice holding her eyes, blood seeping between her fingers. Aliette had not only sliced her face, but she sliced from the top of her right eye downward and across her nose.

In a panic, Aliette broke loose and ran back upstairs. Their mother grabbed all the towels she could, applied pressure with one hand and called for an ambulance with the other.

Patrice underwent extensive surgery in an effort to save her eye, but the cut was too deep. She stayed in the hospital for about three weeks. While she was away, Grace had no choice but to put Aliette out. She didn't know that Aliette already had her new home waiting for her. When Aliette told her this, Grace called her estranged husband, explained what had happened and pleaded with him not to rescue Aliette from this situation. She had put her husband out years before, after suffering his physical and emotional abuse. For once, she asked him to realize his ugly ways and bad habits had ruined their family. They had been instilled into their child, who was now out of control. She begged Aliette's father not to take her in. Since Aliette had chosen the same path as her father, she should suffer the same consequences.

He thought long and hard. He gave into his wife's plea with the hopes that this would lighten her heart of the burden of all the things he had done to her. Maybe then she would feel some sort of comfort. He finally realized the mistakes he had made, and now wouldn't condone or support Aliette's physical abuse toward anyone.

When she heard that her father was supporting her mother's wishes, Aliette just let out a little laugh. She was determined to make it on her own, so at the age of seventeen, she left her mother's house.

To this day, the conversations Aliette had with her mother were just enough to see if everyone was okay. They never spoke about the details of their lives, or the lives of her siblings. It was basically *hello*, *how are you*, and *goodbye*, and it only happened once in a blue moon.

Aliette didn't know even that though her sister still wore a patch over her right eye, she had stopped hating Aliette. Her brother, Manny, felt somewhat responsible for what happened, and he, too, wished Aliette would get herself together. Every now and then, Aliette would call her father, but she was still pretty much on her own.

Aliette took her shower, got dressed, made herself a drink to go and headed over to Sinclair's. The phone call to her family was never made.

Chapter 14
Keeping It Real

The night started off quiet. Sinclair and Aliette were dressed tight! It was 9:00 P.M. by the time they left Sinclair's. While Sinclair was driving, she popped in a CD and decided they would go somewhere different.

Sinclair thought about Wayne as she drove. She felt like she had really accomplished something by telling him what she did about Aliette's past. If he believed everything she had said about Aliette sleeping with her ex-husband, then Aliette was in for a big surprise. There was no way that information wasn't going to start a fight between Aliette and Wayne, and Sinclair couldn't wait to sit back and watch the fireworks. Aliette was a homewrecking bitch, Sinclair thought, and she deserved everything bad that came her way. A smile came over Sinclair's face.

"Okay, so what the hell you smiling about?" Aliette asked as she freshened up her lipstick.

"Nothing. I was just thinking about how you tried to keep Ja'qazz to yourself. You're funny as hell. Now, in less than two weeks, you'll be a married woman. Forget about all of these other men out here, because see, you think you have been tested? Yeah, okay. You and I both know that as a single woman you get play. It's cool, you're feeling it. But as a married woman, you're gonna get mad play."

"I'm gonna always get play, okay?" Aliette informed Sinclair with a diva smile.

"Men are gonna flock to you because men want what they can't have. So your need-to-be-wanted-by-every-man ass will be fulfilled, but without the bullshit because you have a man at home who wants you and has you. You should be glowing, girl, instead of looking all fussed and shit. What's your problem?"

"There is no problem. Just that we need to talk about how I'm going to notify all of the people who are invited to my wedding that there isn't going to be a wedding."

Sinclair slammed on the brakes.

"What?" She turned to face Aliette with her eyes wide with surprise. "Stop playing. What the hell are you talking about? You play too much."

"Wayne sat me down this morning and basically told me that he, or as he put it, *we* haven't been happy for a long time. Then he said that the lack of sex, my nagging and just not showing him love threw him off and out of love with me. The times he was out, he was doing his thing."

"Oh, really?" Sinclair was surprised Wayne had stepped out on Aliette, but not disappointed. Served her right. "So you were right. Ah, did you say get play or get played?"

"Sinclair, not now with your funky-ass remarks."

Sinclair laughed in Aliette's face. She was enjoying this, finally feeling like she was getting the revenge she had waited for so long.

"Alright, I'm sorry. Go ahead," Sinclair said as she covered her mouth to hide a smile that was creeping up.

"He was hanging out with his boys, getting freaky and shit, testing the waters of his manhood with both men and women. Sin, he hooked up with this girl and, well, she's pregnant. She's keeping the baby. All of this was put on my plate this morning. Sick to my stomach was an understatement, and I really could use a drink. Punk ass."

"Oh, shit! You're lying." *But tell me how it feels*, she thought.

Sinclair didn't really know what to say. It was hard for her to pretend the friend role and say supportive things when part of her just wanted to jump up and dance. *Good old Wayne pulled the plug on the dirty water.* She couldn't resist adding a little fuel to the fire.

"Well, I'm not surprised. He had about enough of your shit."

"What do you know about what he had? You say things like you know more about Wayne than you should."

"More than we should? I'm a grown-ass woman. I'll talk to whomever I want." Sinclair remembered vividly how empty she felt when the bomb was dropped on her, but then she also remembered how Aliette told her that she really didn't care that she had ruined the marriage between Vernon and his wife because she didn't know the wife. How could someone be so shallow?

"You got what you deserved," Sinclair announced. "And I've been waiting to say that to you."

They drove the rest of the way in total silence. Sinclair looked over at Aliette. She was crying silently as the tears rolled down her face.

"Don't cry now. The fat man has sung."

"Sinclair, I have to be honest. Sometimes I can't stand you and the shit you say," Aliette told her between sobs.

"And you know what, Aliette? I can't stand your ass either. Trust me, you have no idea how you have impacted my life," Sinclair said as she pulled up to a quaint little spot on Elliott Place and slammed her gear into park. It was an African-American-owned spot where ladies could go to hang out. Guys would come because they knew this was where all of the ladies let their hair down. All kinds of foods were served there. One part was a restaurant lounge and the other had a huge bar.

Sinclair turned the car off and said, "Aliette, not for nothing, but look at what you been doing to Wayne. Look at all of the heartache and torment you put him through in the beginning of your relationship."

"Sinclair, don't lecture me. You don't know shit about my history with Wayne. You only know what I've told you, and that isn't much because you always got something smart to say."

"You didn't think that all of it was going to come to a head if you continued to act like a ho? You think you're the shit and no one has anything on you. Girl, you cute and all, dress nice and shit, but you know what? Men don't like a woman with the air you putting out. Okay? Eventually that shit becomes a turn-off. And to be quite frank—because if I'm not honest with you, no one else will be—you've been getting on my gotdamn nerves too."

"What fucking ever, Sinclair. Where's your man?" Aliette asked as she held her hand to her ear and waited for an answer.

"I kind of had to talk to myself when you flexed about me dating Ja. Where do you get off thinking the world is on Aliette's axis?"

"Sinclair, you knew I was feeling him and you pursued the relationship anyway."

"What is your point?"

"A real woman wouldn't step on her friend's toes just to get a man."

"No, Aliette, a real woman wouldn't fuck another woman's husband. And where's your man now?" Sinclair asked sarcastically. She took a breather. She thought about telling her that Vernon was her husband, but decided to wait. She wondered if Aliette could figure it out by her own stupid self.

"Are we going in or not, because I'm tired of you already. And honestly, I'm ready to go home," Aliette complained.

"Go home to what? I don't know about you, but I'm going in, and I will be having a good-ass time. If you want to leave, I suggest you get to steppin'."

"What the fuck is your problem? I just about had it with your snide, rude comments. If you got some shit on your chest you need to get off, then bitch, I suggest you do it now, because the day I've had has me two seconds off you!"

Ding! Ding! Ding! Ding!

Before Aliette could put one hand on her hip and the other in motion in Sinclair's face, Sinclair punched Aliette right in her mouth.

"Bitch!" Aliette screamed and hit her back. They started fighting in the car. Sinclair held Aliette's hair while she served her uppercuts on a platter. Aliette focused on Sinclair's midsection, saucing her ribs with body jabs. Sinclair managed to get her foot over the console that separated them and started kicking Aliette's legs. Aliette grabbed a fistful of Sinclair's hair.

"Let my hair go, Aliette. I'm not fucking playing with you!

"Hell, no. I'm tired of you, Sinclair, and I'm not done kicking your ass."

With that, Sinclair got her legs back over to her side. With one hand she gripped Aliette's clothes, and with the other, she managed to open her side of the car. It was difficult to swing her legs and hold on to Aliette at the same time, especially since Aliette still had her hair, but she did. Passersby watched as Sinclair started to pull Aliette out of the car.

"C'mon, bitch. You not done kicking my ass? Let me help you out."

Sinclair pulled Aliette out of her seat, over the gear console and out of the car.

"I got your hair, Sinclair. You can't do too much," Aliette said. Sinclair now had Aliette hanging out of the driver's side of the car. Aliette had to let one hand go to the ground to keep what little balance she had, so she wouldn't fall completely on the gravel.

"Wrong move," Sinclair snarled as she kicked Aliette's arm from under her. "I dreamed you got your ass kicked, and would you look at this shit here." By this time, people had gathered and the crowd drew the attention of the bouncer. After a few more blows were exchanged, the bouncer broke them apart.

"You bitch, Sinclair. How you just gonna hit me?"

"You talk too much, Aliette," Sinclair snapped as she tried to reach for Aliette through the bouncer's arms.

"Ladies, squash this or go home." Aliette reached over and got one last hit in. Sinclair caught her with a right that sent her to the ground.

"Ay! I said kill the noise or carry your asses somewhere else tonight. Sistahs is just as bad as these brothas out here, fightin' and shit." The bouncer shook his head in disgust.

"I'm cool," Sinclair said as she patted her hair down as best she could. She could feel her sides hurting, but refused to let Aliette know she had landed a few effective punches. Aliette, on all fours on the ground, not only had a busted lip, but her knees were hurting and she couldn't stand up alone.

"Are you going to leave me down here?" she shouted at the bouncer. He reached down and pulled Aliette up like a rag doll. Sinclair fixed her clothes and Aliette brushed herself off.

"I don't want to hear a word out of either one of you in there," the bouncer warned.

Without saying a word to each other, they headed for the entrance. Both of them wanted to get into the ladies' room to check out what damage had been done.

Before she went to the restroom, Sinclair stopped at the hostess's station to reserve a table. When the hostess asked for a name, Sinclair purposely gave her married name — Vernon's last name. Then she headed to the bathroom where Aliette was already standing in front of a mirror, trying to salvage what she could of her hairstyle. Neither of them spoke as they straightened their hair and reapplied makeup that had been smeared during their fight. They did the best they could then one at a time they left the restroom and headed to the waiting area to be called for a table.

The other customers in the waiting area stared and some even laughed. It seemed like everybody in the place had witnessed their fight.

Sinclair looked back at Aliette who was still adjusting her clothes. *I should beat her ass some more*, she thought.

The hostess called out, "Sinclair Gushon, party of two." Sinclair rose and approached the hostess, ready to be seated. Aliette wasn't sure why Sinclair was getting up, since the hostess had called someone else's last name, but she looked around and saw that no one else in the waiting area was responding to the hostess' announcement.

"You coming?" Sinclair asked Aliette in a gruff voice. She wanted to speak to her as little as possible.

Aliette stood and approached the hostess. They followed her to their table. The chatter of the other customers orchestrated a humming sound, but in the backdrop of it, Aliette kept hearing what the hostess had said. It was low at first, but then it got louder and louder and louder.

Sinclair Gushon, party of two. Sinclair Gushon, party of two. Sinclair Gushon, party of two.

"I know that name," she whispered softly. At least she thought it had been soft.

"I bet you do, tramp," Sinclair answered over her shoulder.

Chapter 15
A Flash from the Past

Sinclair sat at the table and glared at Aliette, who was still trying to put her hair back together after the fight.

I'm not gonna let this tramp ruin my night, Sinclair thought, trying to relax. *Hell, it felt good to punch the shit out of her Get on my damn nerves. Shit, she can let my suits fool her if she wants to, but I bet she know not to mess with me now.*

Momma, I know what you would say right now: "Baby, don't let some ignorant, ill-raised woman ever get you to fighting in the streets It's not ladylike and fighting in the streets is for street people." *Well, Momma, I thank you so much for your lessons that have brought me this far, but — excuse my French — that bitch needed her ass beat a long time ago.*

Sinclair tried to enjoy herself even though her sore ribs were screaming. Since she and Aliette were refusing to speak to each other, there was no sound at the table until Sinclair's cell phone rang.

Aliette rolled her eyes and announced, "I'm going to the bathroom."

Sinclair ignored her and answered her phone. "Hello?"

"Baby girl, what's up? I haven't heard from you all night."

"Ja'qazz. What are you doing?"

"Chillin', baby. How are you doing this evening?"

I'm sitting here with sore ribs and a jacked-up hairdo because I just whipped Aliette's ass. "I'm just having a drink with Aliette. So I see you slipped out quietly Saturday night."

"Yeah. I slipped out after I slipped in. I been at work since six, and it's a pretty dead night. I'm kind of tired. I really want to go home and go to sleep. Ole girl wore my ass out," he said, referring to their sensual lovemaking.

"That's right, bro. Who's your momma?" She forced a laugh. "Well, let me go. Al's coming back from the bathroom and ah . . . well, I'll talk to you later."

"Sinclair, are you alright?"

"Yeah, I'm fine," she responded as she reached into her purse for her Chap Stick and applied it to her lips. She watched Aliette head for the bar.

"Alright, babe. Love you," he said.

"What? What did you say?"

"Sinclair, I'm sorry. I didn't mean—"

"You didn't?"

"Yeah, I guess I did," he admitted. "I love you. Have a nice night."

Sinclair stared at the phone in shock after Ja hung up. Had she heard correctly? She must have. She couldn't blame it on the drinks. She hadn't had any yet.

He loves me? Do I love him? I don't know, but what I do know is I love his stroke, love his lips and his pokey-poke-poke! "I could use some of him right about now," she whispered.

Aliette came back to the table with a drink menu in her hand. She was still pretty upset from everything that had happened to her that day. She wasn't sure she wanted any food, but she had to eat something because she was about to get tore up.

I can't believe I was fighting this hooker in a parking lot. Why she hit me like that is beyond me. I guess she thought she was gonna swing and that was gonna be it. Bet she'll think twice next time. Aliette browsed the menu of wines as she thought about how she would be prepared the next time Sinclair wanted to try some shit like that.

"What are you gonna have?" Aliette asked Sinclair without looking up.

Sinclair ordered her favorite. "Kendall."

Aliette put in the order for the drinks when the waitress came over, then they sat in silence.

Sinclair Gushon. Sinclair Gushon? Sinclair Gushon? Gushon. Gushon. Vernon. Gush. Gushon. Vernon Gushon! Aliette thought. *Is it possible that Sinclair was Vernon Gushon's wife?*

The waitress came back with their wine. Aliette hurriedly grabbed hers.

"Damn, this shit is good," Aliette said, drinking half the glass in one gulp. She waved for the waitress to bring another round. Sinclair just looked at her and knew that by the end of the night, Aliette would be drunk and she would need to be carried out of there. When the waitress came with two more glasses of wine, Sinclair tried to tell her she didn't want another glass, but Aliette told the waitress not to worry about it, she would drink it later. Before she let the waitress go, she asked her to bring her two double shots of tequila.

"Oh yeah, it's on now," Sinclair said. "Don't get brave from those shots and get it again," Sinclair warned. Aliette didn't respond.

It was an awkward situation for both of them. Finally they were face-to-face, Sinclair unmasked of the secret that she was Vernon's ex-wife. Aliette was face-to-face with a woman who, when they met, was crying over something Aliette had done. Neither one of them knew what the other had been stripped of and burdened with because of this situation. There was no friendship going on at that table.

The lounge was packed by then and despite their jacked-up appearance, they were both still getting eyes from the men. Neither of them minded because it took their attention away from the tense mood at the table.

Aliette had begun to sway and bop in her seat when she was approached by a brotha who asked her to dance. At the same time, the waitress brought her the shots of tequila. She downed the shots and ordered another round. *They'll kick in soon,* she thought, hoping the shots would numb the pain she was feeling in her legs. She accepted his offer and led the way to the dance floor.

In little to no time, Aliette was on one of the tables, doing her thing. Sinclair kept her eyes on Aliette because she knew she was juiced up and it was only a matter of time before Aliette fell. Sinclair wanted to see it, frame by frame. But the girl was bad, Sinclair had to admit, and by the time Aliette was done she had enough dollar bills from the onlookers to pay for the tab.

"Whew, girl, that was fun! Did you see me up there? I forgot I could do all that stuff. Tell me, how did I look? Did I look good? Was I cute, girl? Tell me!" Aliette slurred drunkenly.

Sinclair said nothing. She looked Aliette in the eye and said absolutely nothing.

"What? What's wrong now? What now, you gonna try to left hook me or something?"

Still, Sinclair said nothing.

"You know what, Sinclair? Go ahead and sit there and sulk. We had a fight. So what? All friends have fights, and if they're true friends, they get over it. You've wanted to hit me for a long time. I could feel it. You finally did it, I fought your ass back, and now we're here, two sistahs with messed-up hair and hurting bones, 'cause I know I got a few in on you, too, now."

It was time for Sinclair to confess. "Aliette, we're not really friends. When we met in the park, I knew exactly who you were. Your face had been embedded in my mind ever since I got those pictures of you, Vernon and that other trick."

"I know who you are too. Well, I know now." Aliette was trying to play it cool, like she wasn't surprised by Sinclair's true identity.

"Yup, and all I wanted was revenge. How do you think Wayne knew you were at Barry's that afternoon?"

"You told him?"

"You slept with my husband?"

"You told him I was there with Ja?"

"You had my husband's dick in your mouth and sucked it like it was a Rocket Pop?"

"And you call me a liar?"

"When you sleep with another woman's husband, you start shit, okay? And it gets better. I told Wayne everything," Sinclair said as she twisted her neck.

"What do you mean everything?"

"Ev-er-y-thang." Sinclair dragged out each syllable to be sure Aliette understood she meant she had revealed all of Aliette's dirt to Wayne. She snapped her hand out to Aliette and back like she was snapping her with a whip.

Aliette was fuming. She wanted to punch Sinclair in the mouth this time. Without realizing it, she stood and pulled her arm back to do just that.

"Come on with it, Aliette, because I got a half a can of whoopass left. Your best bet would be to sit down," Sinclair threatened as she watched Aliette's drunk ass sway back and forth.

Aliette retreated to her chair and put her arms on her lap. The tension was impenetrable. As they sat each sipping on their drinks, someone tapped Sinclair on her shoulder. She looked up and was speechless. Aliette stayed focused on Sinclair a moment longer, but then she looked up too. She turned so pale it looked like a bucket of white paint had been dumped over her face. Almost choking on her wine, Aliette swallowed what she had in her mouth. Sinclair stood, and turned so she was face-to-face with Vernon.

"Sinclair?"

Because she couldn't open her mouth to speak, Sinclair just stood there. Her mind was running in overdrive.

"Well, well, motherfucking well," she said. "Long time no see, Vernon Gushon."

He looked okay. Nice suit, coif was tight, and still had his own teeth, from what she could see through that slight and unsure smile of his. Her palms were sweaty. She clenched her fists, but then drew her arms behind her as if she was hiding something. She had to do this, because if she didn't, he would be eating those teeth.

Sinclair turned to look at Aliette. By then she had gotten a little bit of her color back, but her expression revealed no emotion. Vernon also looked at Aliette and realized with whom Sinclair was dining. His mouth practically dropped to the floor. Furrowing her eyebrows, Sinclair looked at Aliette then back at Vernon. One was as white as a ghost, and the other had his mouth hanging open with the stupidest expression on his face. Since no one was going to say anything, Sinclair thought she would start and finish.

"Hello . . ." She paused. "Vernon."

Aliette tossed back the last of her wine and looked at Vernon. Sinclair could feel them staring at each other though she kept focused on Vernon. As Vernon finally began to speak, Aliette felt his hesitance. His eyes were shifting back and forth in an obvious attempt to communicate with Aliette. He was pleading with her to keep quiet.

"Sin. Sinclair, it's been some time." He looked at her, yet past her, to keep his eye on Aliette.

Is that all he can say? Sincliar was laughing inside. *I would hate to be the set of balls sweating between that ass right about now*, she thought. *P fucking U.* She turned back around, sat down and stared Aliette right in her face. Aliette followed her every move and tried not to look at Vernon. As difficult as it was, she managed to keep her eyes on Sinclair. She could see Sinclair was getting fired up again.

"Vernon, let me introduce you to Aliette."
Sinclair released a short, fake laugh. "Oh, my bad.
You two already know each other."

"Sinclair, I don't know what you're talking
about," Vernon responded.

Sinclair got back up and in his face.

"You would stand here and try to lie in my
face again when I'm sitting here with one of your
fuck partners, Vernon? You are still an asshole."

"Aliette?" Vernon looked to her, hoping for
some support.

"Bro, I got my own shit going on right now.
I'm just as shocked as you are, so don't Aliette me,"
she answered.

Sinclair sat back down with a satisfied smile.

As Sinclair sat in front of Aliette, she
remembered the pictures Aliette had taken of her in
the park. That was one of the worst days of
Sinclair's life, and Aliette had captured it. Sinclair
also remembered, as she turned back to Vernon,
sitting on her couch and looking at pictures of the
two of them fucking.

Vernon already knew the deal. He knew
exactly who Aliette was and he now knew that
Sinclair knew who she was too. Everyone in this
triangle of deception knew exactly what time it was.
Aliette knew she had been with him in a threesome
a year ago and that he got divorced behind it.
Vernon knew Aliette had sucked his dick while
another woman was sucking her pussy while he was
married to Sinclair. And Sinclair knew Aliette was
the woman in the picture, choking her then
husband's chicken like she was his mother hen,
while some other hooker ate her rot twat.

While Vernon stood there, he stared at Aliette, who refused to take her eyes off Sinclair to look up at him. Her gut was telling her not to. He held up a matchbook and pretended to sneeze. Aliette took that opportunity to look up and read the matchbook as Sinclair reached for her glass of wine. It was from the hotel where he was staying. He held his hand near his face, mimicking a telephone. He wanted Aliette to call him. She looked back at Sinclair and pretended she hadn't seen his gesture.

"Sinclair, maybe we can talk while I'm in town," Vernon said.

"Fuck you, Vernon. I don't think so."

Once, 361 days ago, Sinclair woke up as she did every day before that one. She got dressed, probably ate something and went to get the mail. She thumbed through the junk mail and went right for the manila envelope with the words DO NOT BEND stamped on it. That day, Sinclair's life changed. Her world was turned upside down and pieces to her life puzzle were taken away and discarded, never to be found again — until this moment.

The silence was so loud. Sinclair looked at Aliette, smiled softly, and shook her head. It felt good to be controlling this situation. Neither Vernon nor Aliette knew what she was thinking; they didn't know what she would do next.

Aliette sighed because she didn't know what else to do. She accepted the dare from her conscience and asked Sinclair if she was alright. "Sinclair, are you going to be okay?"

Sinclair was receiving her words, but they were coming to her very slowly. Everything around her seemed to be moving in slow motion. Her adrenaline was thick and flowing rapidly through her veins. She shook her head again because Aliette was still trying to act like she had her best interest at heart.

"What the fuck is it to you? No! I'm not okay." She turned to walk away, and Vernon grabbed her arm.

Ding! Ding! Ding!

Smack! The palm of Sinclair's hand found Vernon's face. Sinclair glared at Aliette then made her way to the ladies' room.

Aliette's eyes followed her then she turned in Vernon's direction. She started to get up to go over to him, but he shook his head while he rubbed his face. He knew that would be the wrong thing to do. If Sinclair came out and saw them talking, all hell would break loose.

"Look, Aliette, I'm gonna be over by the bar. You know where I'm staying if you want to call me later." He walked away, leaving Aliette, still drunk, shocked and confused, at the table.

Splashing cold water on her face, a few tears found their way out of Sinclair's eyes. She hadn't seen Vernon since their divorce. She'd never imagined seeing him again—not this way, for sure. But now, seeing Vernon again had made her more upset than she would have imagined, and she knew this could only mean one of two things: either she still needed to get some things off her chest, or she was still in love with him. Cringing at the thought of the latter, she looked at herself in the mirror and saw a whole bunch of unanswered questions.

Now that she had finally revealed her secret to Aliette she felt like she had some sort of revenge. Still, she didn't feel any closure. The whole thing would have to be discussed with both of them. This was the only way she could truly begin healing. She realized she had a long way to go, and it was going to be messy.

She dried her face off, and while she was touching up her makeup, she decided she wasn't going to sit there and be a spectacle to either one of them. Besides, she still had half a can of whoopass left and was ready to serve it up to the next opponent.

When she returned to the table, Aliette was sipping on some water with lemon.

"I'm leaving," Sinclair stated as she drank her last bit of wine and turned around to leave.

"Sinclair, wait. Why? Now that we're all here, let's just try and talk about it. I really need to talk about it."

"Aliette, this shit ain't about you. You and Vernon act like I did this shit to y'all, but it was you guys who fucked me dry. You fucked Vernon, and he fucked you. You know, I've never said this to anyone, but I truly hate you. We were never friends, and we will never be friends."

Aliette made the second biggest mistake of her life. She grabbed Sinclair's arm.

Ding! Ding!

Sinclair hauled off and slapped Aliette so hard Aliette's neck snapped back. Vernon came running over.

"Come on. You could be next if you want!" Sinclair taunted. She held her hands up like she had defeated Aliette in the pre-fight. Vernon was her title fight for the night.

"Okay, Sinclair. I'm backing off," he said as calmly as he could.

Sinclair was shaking. Her eyes were blood-shot.

"How am I supposed to get home, Sinclair?" Aliette yelled as Sinclair started to walk to the door.

"The best way you know how, you drunk bitch. Ask Vernon if you can get another ride." Sinclair stood straight, held her head up and walked out of the lounge. Vernon looked at Aliette then walked out behind Sinclair.

"Oh no you didn't!" Aliette yelled to Vernon. "Run behind her? What about me?"

A feeling of great remorse came over Vernon as he watched Sinclair get into the car. He remembered the day she had thrown him out. He had come home from work and she was sitting on the couch with the pictures scattered across the coffee table. He could tell she had been crying because her normally thin and flawless face was swollen and blotchy. Looking him straight in the eye, she told him he had taken his vows in vain. He deceived her, possibly exposed her to sexually transmitted diseases and totally disrespected her as a woman and his wife. Sinclair was so irate she didn't give him a chance to say anything. Seeing photos of him in the act had put her over the edge.

While he stood in the parking lot alone, Vernon regretted he didn't have the opportunity to at least apologize to Sinclair. Right after he left, she had divorce papers drawn up. He was served via certified mail a week later. Anything that was disputed was done through their lawyer. There was no personal contact between them. They hadn't spoken after that. He had tried to call her several times, but she neither answered her phone nor returned his calls. After a while, he just stopped trying. The love she had for him was strong, because when Sinclair loved she did it hard and unconditionally. When she finally cut him off, he knew he had broken her heart.

Chapter 16
Prayer Is, Pleasure Is . . .

As Sinclair walked in the house, she checked her messages. There were none. She was so tired. All she wanted to do was get in the shower and go to bed. She was still feeling the shock of seeing Vernon at the lounge. *That motherfucka,* she thought.

She slipped into the bathroom and headed straight for the shower. She thought about looking at the pictures, but as soon as the silly thought came into her mind, it went out. *I don't need to see that shit.*

After she took her shower, she took some aspirin and climbed into bed. She needed answers, and who better to ask than the big man above.

Dear God,

Okay, you already know this situation because You created it for me. I just need some questions answered, and once I know the answers, I believe I can get on with my life. I need to know why this happened to me. Momma raised me to see the signs of deception. Why didn't I see them in Vernon? I didn't even see it when I had all the signs right in my gotdamn face. Ah, sorry. I said "gotdamn" and that ain't You.

Anyhow, why did I allow myself to be pulled in by the need to get revenge? Momma said what goes around comes around, and whoever did you wrong would get theirs one day. I loved my husband. Nobody's perfect, but I was committed to him and the vows I took before You. I accepted him and his faults. Why couldn't he do the same for me? You put it in my face and I still didn't see it. Was it because deep down I was just as capable of being a deceiver as Vernon and Aliette were?

These last several months, I woke up every day and looked for the opportunity to get back at Aliette with open arms and a smile on my face, so I guess I am just like them. Am I the same as them, God? Yes, I am, and You know what, God? You made me this way. I was alone, and okay being alone, dealing with my issues all by my self. But one day You decided to send her my way. What's up with that?

Yeah, You have a standing appointment to show up anytime You damn well please, but that heifer didn't, and she still don't. Yeah, I said it. You of all people had to know how this was gonna go down, so don't even try it. Why? Is there a lesson somewhere in here I need to learn because all I've learned so far is that I've got a mean right uppercut and the potential to be a deceiving and dishonest person.

Then there is Ja'qazz. Obviously, we were meant to meet because You wouldn't have brought us together that sunny day if we weren't. Anyhow, Ja wanted to meet me, but Aliette, drowning in her fantasy of them together, never gave him the opportunity. Now, I'm no scientist, but how can she feel that it was okay not to tell me this and then be all mad when she finds out I've also deceived her? The same way she was with Vernon and didn't care was the same way she didn't care about anything but having Ja all to herself. So I got with Ja at first just for one more way to piss off Aliette, but did You mean for my relationship with him to be more than that?

I don't know what I'm supposed to do with Ja. I mean, I plan to ride the wave and see if we can be together, but damn, I really wonder what lesson You got hidden in the wings for me with that.

Last but certainly not least, why did You bring Vernon to me? What else could I have to say to him? When I had the chance, I couldn't say anything, and that was Your doing, too, You know. Why did he even approach me, not knowing how I was going to react? Did You give him a new set of balls because the wimp wasn't wearing those when I threw him out that day. Well, whatever Your reasons are, I accept them, but I can't say that I won't curse and carry on while dealing with them. So I'm apologizing now, and I hope You forgive me, 'cause it's about to get really ugly.

I ask that You keep Your hand over me and my momma, may she rest in peace. I miss her so much. She should be here with me now. She would know exactly how to handle this. Oh, and Ja'qazz, he's going to have a hard way with me. Watch over the homeless, the hungry and the less fortunate. I guess I better mention Vernon and Aliette, too, because . . . well, I don't really know why. Please, please guide me to do what is right, ultimately, for me. Amen.

This was not the first time Sinclair had prayed, but like most people, it was only when she needed something or wanted help with something that she called on God. She vowed from that day forward that she would take the time to sit and talk to the Greater One just to keep up on things. She believed she didn't have to be in a church to pray to God, and decided she would transform some part of her place to represent her quiet space and the space where she would get in touch. She fell asleep with these peaceful thoughts.

As she drifted off to sleep, she asked herself if she had really rid herself of Vernon. After all, she was still living in the same house they had lived in as husband and wife, and seeing him that night had brought back emotions. If she was over him, there should be no emotions, at least not like the emotions she felt. Could it be because of his deep brown eyes? Could it be his chiseled chest where he held her close when she would cry? Could it be his hands that cupped her butt and hips, moving them until he released himself inside her? Who knew? All she knew was that seeing him brought questions, and they needed answers, or else she couldn't move forward.

Moving slowly on her freshly washed satin sheets, she felt herself getting aroused from these thoughts of him. She wanted to fight it, but then resisted no more. She allowed her mind to run through the maze of their relationship, telling every story again and again, making her conscience second-guess itself. Her torso was pulsating and her back arched when she reached the point of ecstasy. Coming down and still half-asleep, she gave a cry of submission.

Monday was scary. Sinclair was tired, even though she had gotten plenty of rest. Holding a cup of coffee, she walked into her office. Her phone rang. She answered it.

"Sinclair speaking."

"Hey, Sin, it's Ja."

"Hey, you. What's happening? Did you get some sleep last night? I remember you saying it was slow and you were trying to get out early."

"No. Not really. Sinclair, can we talk, or are you busy right now?"

"Well, it is Monday, and I did just get into the office. What about dinner? Let's say around seven?"

"Cool, I'll pick you up from your place."

"Right. See you then."

Sinclair hung up the phone. She couldn't help but think about the questions for which she wanted answers. Maybe today she would know why Ja'qazz came into her life. It had been about a week since they started seeing each other, and they hadn't really actually defined it as that. He slipped and said he loved her, but how could he love her in such little time, and what was it about her that he loved? As she rubbed her head, she thought that would be a good topic for discussion over dinner.

Chapter 17
Make Light with Laughter

As Aliette sat in her bedroom, more than hung over, she realized that in a few months the rent Wayne had set aside would be depleted and that she would either have to get a roommate or get a full-time job. She hadn't worked a full forty-hour week in so long, but those were her only two options. There was no way she could move in with Sinclair. She had her own things going on, and right then, they weren't friends.

The night before was something. Never in her wildest dreams did Aliette think she would see Vernon again. *And Sinclair! That bitch lost her mind.* Still, no matter how Sinclair had gone off on her, Aliette had to admit Sinclair did have a right to be angry. Somehow, Aliette was determined to straighten this whole thing out.

As she got out of bed, she decided it would be best to talk to Vernon first, instead of trying to call Sinclair. She called the number to the hotel she had seen on the matchbook.

"How may I direct your call?" the hotel employee asked after answering.

"Vernon Gushon's room, please."

"Mr. Gushon," Vernon answered.

"Vernon, it's Aliette." She didn't waste any time with small talk. "What are you doing in town? Whew! There was some uncool shit last night. I knew you got divorced behind our fling, but I had no idea until last night that Sinclair was your ex-wife."

"What?"

"I swear. We just actually met about six months ago."

"And she never said anything to you about being married before?"

"Well, yeah, but she never told me a name or the reason why she divorced."

"So you've been just friends?"

She was quiet. Tiny red dots were flashing before her eyes, and she broke out in a sweat. *It must be all that liquor. But damn, could I use a drink now.*

"I don't think we're friends any longer."

"Why not?"

"Vernon, why the hell do you think?"

"Well, what happened?"

"You know what? Let's meet for dinner or something and talk more."

"Alright, where?"

"Come to my place around nine tonight."

"Alright. Give me your address."

"It's 247 Darien Boulevard in Thousand Oaks. I'll call you to confirm. Bye."

"Later."

As she hung up the phone in utter disbelief, she ran to her box and got the picture of Sinclair in the park and the set of pictures her ex-husband had received in the mail. She had never entered Sinclair's photo in the contest as she had planned because there was something so private about the moment she was having. Aliette felt privileged to have had the opportunity to witness it.

Looking at the photo now, Sinclair was clearly in total distress. Her eyes told her story, but Aliette just didn't get it. *I get it now, Sinclair, and I ain't that mad at you.* She shook her head as she sat on the edge of her couch, finally embarrassed for what she'd done.

She has held this in all of this time and never told me who she was. Why? You'd think that would be the first thing a woman would do when she met up with her husband's mistress. And now that I really think about it, she did say things that should've told me she had issues with me. What am I supposed to do now? She knew who I was from day one. I remember Vernon telling me she sent copies of the pictures to the spouses of everybody who was in them. That would mean she allowed me to be her friend nonetheless, probably to get me back somehow, she thought.

All of a sudden, her embarrassment turned into a feeling of deceit. She couldn't believe Sinclair would be her friend with this situation heavy on her heart. She wanted to know why.

Aliette picked up the phone and called Sinclair.

"Morning, Sinclair speaking."

"Sinclair, Aliette. I need to talk to you. Ah, it's really important."

"I don't have anything to say to you, Al."

"Well, think of something quick because I'm on my way to your office."

Aliette hung up the phone without saying good-bye. She got in the shower then got dressed, grabbed the picture of Sinclair crying in the park, the pictures of Vernon and her with the other woman — *I knew I kept these for a reason* — and her purse, and was out the door. As she drove, she chuckled. Wondering how long Sinclair had planned on keeping up this charade was making her laugh. Shit, they had been friends for six months, and if Sinclair hadn't used her married name that night, she might still have been keeping her secret. Sinclair was damn sure hell-bent on getting revenge.

And that bitch did. She told Wayne everything. That's why he broke off our engagement. This put Aliette in her "oh, I don't think so" mode. When she confronted Sinclair, Aliette wasn't going to let her accuse her of breaking up Sinclair's marriage with Vernon. Obviously he was unhappy before their fling if he was so ready to jump into bed with two other chicks. Aliette was ready for any shit Sinclair was going to throw. As she pulled up in front of Sinclair's office, Aliette could see her sitting at her desk.

"All poised and shit, thinking she don't have no issues. Look at her. Well, I guess this conversation is long overdue, and I'm so ready," she said as she got out of the car and headed for the office.

"What do you want, Aliette?"

Aliette threw the picture of her in the park down on her desk.

"You wanna go there, huh?" Sinclair said, looking at the picture.

Then Aliette threw the pictures of Vernon, the other woman and her on the desk.

Sinclair stared at them. Minutes went by before either one said anything. Finally, Aliette moved toward a chair.

"Don't get comfortable, Aliette. You're not staying too long."

"How long were you going to let this go on, Sinclair? Here I am thinking that we're friends and you keep this from me. All these months of hanging out, having girl talk, confiding in you about my extracurricular activities, and you've known all along who I was. You didn't feel the need to tell me that you knew who I was before last night?"

"Aliette, I don't think this is the time or place to have this conversation. This is a bit much, and I need a few to get it together, okay?" she responded in a voice of warning.

"Get it together? What do you need to get together?" Her tone was now tight and harsh.

"Al, I'm telling you in the nicest manner I know how to right now, back the fuck off!"

"Fuck you. You walk around here like you are the fucking Queen of England, giving advice and reading people like they're the *Daily News*, but you got shit of your own. Girl, please. No need to front any longer."

Sinclair walked over and closed the door. Aliette winced as Sinclair walked past her, not taking her eyes off her. Sinclair took her seat and slowly folded her hands in front of her.

"As much as I want to kick your ass right now, my job is much more important, and since you're not going to let this go, even though I told you that we should talk later, let's get this shit over with. When I was in the park crying because I was alone and still very distraught about divorcing my husband, the man I loved unconditionally, you were taking candid shots of people, including me. When

I realized who you were, I had two options: I could have either kicked your funky ass like I want to do now or I could have said nothing. I chose to say nothing."

"That shit doesn't make sense, Sinclair. I would have handed you your ass right then and there."

Sinclair got up and paced around her desk as she continued. "In the beginning, I had big plans for you. I had it mapped out how I was going to bring you to your lowest, like I was on that sunny day in the park. See—" she held the picture just an inch away from Aliette's face—"I remember it very clearly. There were times where I could have brought it up but chose not to. I figured in time, I would get the nerve. But then opportunity kept knocking. You were so wrapped up in you, you didn't hear me telling you I knew who you were. The only thing I never came right out and told you was who my ex-husband was and why I was divorced. I don't know what he told you about me, if he told you anything at all, and I really don't care. I had divorced him, he moved back to Wheeling, and I was moving on with my life. For whatever reason, you and I met, and here the fuck we are.

"See, the difference between you and me is that I have learned to play the cards I'm dealt while you continuously bitch about your cards. You're always a victim of someone else's circumstance. You came into my office under the impression that I had lied to you or didn't tell you something about me you felt you should have known. Why should I have told you? You already knew you ruined some woman's marriage. When you explained how it all went down, you know what I got from your version of the story? You couldn't have cared less who you hurt, as long as you were okay in the end. You use people to aid you along in your selfish life, thinking it will ease the pain you feel in your lonely insides. Talk about creating bad karma.

"Let me ask you something: What's up with your family? When was the last time you talked to your mother?" Sinclair folded her arms across her chest and waited for a response.

"For your information—" Aliette started to answer.

"Didn't think so. And why did Wayne leave you for real? Let me help you out. You're a ho. You cheated on him and totally disrespected him as a man. Any chance you got, you rode his back, complained about things he did and didn't do around your house. You totally cut him off sexually because nine times out of ten you slept with someone else on your way home. So you see, I didn't have to handle you, per se, because you were being handled. I believe what comes around goes around, and you're now a very lonely woman. I was the only friend you had, Aliette."

"Friend? I don't need a friend like you, Sinclair."

"You're right. I thought about this just last night. I asked myself how we could ever be friends with this hovering over my head. I prayed for guidance because I needed to get this resolved but didn't know how to go about it. Lo and behold, you came to me with it. Thank you, bitch." Sinclair sat back down.

Tears made their way down Aliette's face. The strong woman who had walked through the door ten minutes before now felt like she was small enough to swing her ankles off a dime. The woman who she herself had deceived a year ago, had reduced her verbally, after showing her what it felt like to be the receiver of deceit. Without notice, she started to cry uncontrollably.

"Save it for the next show. I'm so not interested. From experience, I know your pain, but as a scorned woman, I could give a shit about your tears. And not only have you wrecked my marriage, but you wrecked yours before you even walked down the aisle."

"Fucking tell me about it, Sinclair. How dare you talk to my fiancé without my knowing?"

"Aliette, the way I had it in for you, you're lucky I didn't mess around and fuck the shit out of him and have his baby just out of spite."

"Yeah, you would do some foul shit like that."

"We'll never know because it looks like someone else beat me to the punch," Sinclair said with a wicked laugh.

"I just can't believe this shit," Aliette said.

"Look, let me make this quick. I suggest you seek some counseling, especially with what just happened with Wayne. You should start getting yourself together. You need to reach out to your family also because as of right now, you have no one. Family is forever, and they have to deal with your bullshit. Try to concentrate on you. Spend some time with yourself and try to find inner peace. Go away for a while, like a personal retreat or something. I don't know. All I know is I feel better, and thank you for saving me the trouble of having to bring this up to you. Now, if you don't mind, I have some work to do."

Sinclair stood in front of her desk and watched Aliette get up and walk out of her office. Letting out a big sigh of relief, she sat down and leaned back in her leather swivel chair. Fighting the tears, she accepted this was an answer to one of the questions in her heart, and it was okay.

Now that she had a banging headache, work was the last place she wanted to be. She decided to take an early lunch and take a drive. The sun wasn't out. In fact, it was a very gray and dull day.

Chapter 18
Ma and Me

Unsure where she was going, Sinclair found herself reminiscing about her mother. When Sinclair was growing up, her mother always told her when someone lies, they can't love the person they lie to. They're lying because they love themselves more, and they have to make sure they'll be okay first; they cover their tracks and think about that other person later.

Baby, a lie can spoil the foundation of any relationship. Even if the person who lied to you was your husband, you may still love him, but the day will come when he will tell a lie that will make you cut him loose. You both may be alone, but being alone ain't so bad.

Sinclair began to cry. *I know, Momma, I did. I let him go, but I'm gonna be okay by myself.*

Her mother had also taught her lessons that helped Sinclair understand her situation with Aliette. *Sinclair, the best way to let a person know they've done something to cause you problems is to tell them politely; better yet, sometimes saying nothing is the best solution. The offending person will notice your silence and think about what happened to cause it.*

Sinclair realized she had expended so much energy trying to get revenge on Aliette, but in the end, it was Sinclair's silence and distance in their friendship that caused Aliette to think about things and realize something was wrong. It hadn't really been necessary for Sinclair to plan out some elaborate revenge because, in the end, Aliette put things together on her own, and her own bad behavior brought about the unhappy things that were now happening in her life.

Sinclair's mother, Genevieve Pinault, had taught her many useful lessons, and she was Sinclair's idol. As she reminisced about her mother, Sinclair remembered her scent; her face cream made her smell of fresh-cut roses.

Born and raised in the south of France, Genevieve moved to New Jersey during her high school years and graduated with a bachelor's degree in business administration from a local community college. She later went on to open her own company, preparing legal documents for people at a nominal price. This was her own business, and she was very proud of it.

Then she wed Sinclair's father, Randy Welch. Theirs was not a happy marriage. Genevieve would work countless hours of overtime to avoid being home with him since all they did was argue. He never would say what made him angry, but Genevieve suspected it was because she held her own and never asked him for anything. She paid all the bills, she bought the food, she bought Sinclair's clothes; it seemed all he did was occupy space in the house and fuss. After a while, Genevieve got tired of it. She knew it took two to argue, so Gene, as her friends and family called her, would ignore him as if he wasn't there any time he tried to start a fight. This would make him even angrier.

One day, Gene came home for lunch. She received an anonymous phone call. The voice on the other end told her to go to a local restaurant, Spades, where she would find her husband. Not paying too much attention to it, she decided she wasn't going to cut her lunch short just to see what that fool Randy was doing this time. She finished her lunch, brushed her teeth, washed her face then finally went over to Spades. When she pulled up, she saw Randy's car in the parking lot. She got out of her car and walked over to his. As she got closer, she could see there were four people in the car.

Gene knocked on the window and Randy opened it. She could see from the look in his eyes that he was not sober. He, along with three girls who were barely fifteen years old, had been shooting up. Words couldn't explain how Gene felt, although she wasn't surprised.

She decided right there that she would forgive him. There was no reason to be angry. Call it a blessing in disguise; he had given her a reason to let him go for good. She turned around and started to walk away, but then she turned back around, walked back to the car and grabbed the keys. After all, it was her car he was driving.

Gene went back to work and called the locksmith to have the locks changed at the house. She had a new key delivered to her job. When she got home, Randy was waiting on the stairs, looking sorry.

At that very moment, Gene looked at Randy and couldn't for the life of her see what it was he represented. He couldn't or wouldn't keep a job.

She was unsure which reason it was. All he did was eat, sleep and have a party on her nerves.

Shaking her head in disgust, she told him he was out. She wasn't going to tolerate his mess any longer, and he had to leave. Life was too short to be unhappy.

"Even if the person who lied to you was your husband, you may love him, but the day will come when he will tell a lie that will make you cut him loose." Sinclair nodded in agreement with her mother's words. It felt as if Gene were sitting in the passenger's seat of Sinclair's car.

After Randy was gone, it was just Gene and Sinclair, and they had to take care of each other. The end of the year was coming, and each summer, Sinclair would go down south to visit her grandparents. That year, her mother decided they needed a vacation together and they would fly to Arizona. It was a two-week vacation that Sinclair would never forget. They went to the Grand Canyon and did lots of shopping. They even brought back one of those fireplaces made out of cooked clay. It sat in the back on their patio.

Shortly after they returned, Gene was feeling tired all time and her stomach was always cramping. She went to the doctor. After a quick exam, he told her either she was pregnant or she had a virus. He did blood work on her, though, and it came back positive for Hepatitis B. She was devastated as there was no cure, just preventative recourse for this disease.

In the beginning, she was fine. She took the prescribed medication and adjusted her diet, but after two years, that wasn't enough. Her liver had become inflamed and she was immediately put on a list to receive a transplant.

This was very difficult for Sinclair. Here she was in the prime of her teenage years and she was losing her mother.

Gene managed to hold on until Sinclair was about seventeen years old. A week before Sinclair was to graduate, her mother passed away, having never received a liver transplant. Sinclair had no one. She had no idea how she was going to survive alone. The funeral director had been a client of Gene's, so he did the funeral on credit until Sinclair received any insurance monies her mother had left.

Sinclair went to a lawyer and explained her situation. She advised him that she was the sole beneficiary of her mother's business. It had no liabilities. She owned it straight out and it was doing very well. He looked at this as an opportunity to grow his firm and bought it from her for $50,000. When the deal was sealed and Sinclair got paid for her mother's business, she used it along with the insurance money to pay for her mother's funeral, then paid off the balance on the mortgage.

There wasn't enough money left for Sinclair to go to a four-year college, so she stayed in the house and went to a local community college while working part time. The little that was left over was enough to give her mother the most beautiful headstone, specially made for her. Engraved on it were lines from a poem Sinclair had written for her mother.

Rose-scented cheeks I kissed every day

We held hands every night when we prayed
A life not chosen but lived and loved
I now surrender you to our Father above

I love you, Mommy

Sinclair knelt down in front of her mother's headstone and touched it with grace. She cried and wished her mother were there to hug her and tell her everything was going to be okay. She knew this already, but she wanted to hear it in her mother's voice and smell her rose-scented face. She wanted to feel her mother's hands softly pinching her cheeks. She wanted to lay down on her mother's lap while she brushed her hair and told her about life as it was and would be for her. Sinclair wanted to play double-dutch, hopscotch and jacks with her mother. She wanted her best friend in the whole wide world.

Realizing that she was being selfish, she reminded herself that she had her mother in spirit. She was the woman she was today because of her mother, and she was very thankful. From that day forward, Sinclair promised herself she would make weekly trips to visit her mother, each time bringing fresh-cut roses and placing them on her grave.

A sense of peace filled Sinclair. There never was a doubt that her mother loved her. Her mother made sure she had everything she needed and told her every day she loved her. Sinclair was never put on the back burner for anything, and because now it had been some time since she had been to visit her mother, Sinclair felt guilty. Her heart wasn't heavy, though, because she knew her mother had the gift of forgiveness. She had passed it on to Sinclair.

Her mother had taught her about forgiveness after she put Randy out. Sinclair couldn't understand why her mother had never cried; she never seemed angry about what her husband had done. Her mother had told her: *"Sinclair, sometimes people can't love because they don't love themselves. There's no need to be angry or seek revenge. They'll be the ones who have to live with their actions."* Sinclair had learned this lesson at a young age, and as she sat beside her mother's grave remembering what her mother had taught her, she realized that now more than ever she needed to focus on forgiveness.

She sat in the cemetery for about two hours, then Sinclair gathered herself and went back to the office. She finished her work and called it a night. Her spirit was feeling renewed, and she was looking forward to dinner with Ja'qazz.

When she walked into the house, the first thing she did was look around. She took a deep breath and accepted the reality that she was still living in the past. She had the same furniture, dishes, pictures, linen, and car she had when she was with Vernon. He was the only thing missing. Well, not missing, but gone. And that was the answer to another one of her questions: She couldn't really be over him if she still lived in his essence.

Sinclair took off her clothes then checked the answering machine. There was one message.

"Sinclair, baby, I'll be there at seven like I promised."

She smiled at the sound of Ja's voice and went into the bedroom to prepare for her night.

Chapter 19
Seeing Is Believing

As Aliette sat in her car in front of her house, she angrily relived what had just happened. She pulled out the fifth of Jack Daniel's that she had picked up after leaving Sinclair's office and took a long swig, wiping her mouth with the back of her hand and letting out a silent burp. She took another swig, drooling a bit because it was too much.

As she wiped her mouth again, she looked in the direction of her house and saw Wayne pulling up. She slouched low in her seat so he wouldn't see her when he got out of his car. Wayne didn't even look in the direction of her car; he stepped out and walked to the passenger's side. He opened the door and a woman got out and followed him into the house. Not wanting to believe her eyes, Aliette took another swig. She was getting angrier by the minute.

"Bastard!" she yelled. "That's my fucking house!" She got out of the car and went into the house.

"Wayne, you punk, who the hell do you have in my fucking house?" she shouted as she entered.

Wayne came running out of the bedroom and immediately grabbed her. "Aliette, what is your problem?" he demanded.

"What the hell do you think you're doing, bringing some bitch in my house?"

"Aliette, she's here to help me move some of my things. I told you I was going to come and get some of my stuff." Wayne was trying to stay calm.

"I don't care. Where is she?" Aliette tried to break loose from Wayne, but he held her tight.

"Don't, Aliette. She's just a friend. She has nothing to do with this."

"She gotta come out, Wayne, and this is the only way."

"Mia," Wayne yelled out, "go get in the car." A moment later, Mia came out and jetted past Aliette with her face covered. Aliette fought vigorously to break free from Wayne and get to her.

"You're not getting loose, so you need to chill," Wayne said.

Aliette was so angry. She started to try to hit Wayne, but she couldn't get her hands free.

When Mia was safely out of the house, Wayne released Aliette and pushed her away. "I'll be back another time for the rest of my things."

"Fuck you, Wayne. And you better not bring that bitch back with you."

"You got issues, Aliette." Wayne walked out backward. He didn't trust Aliette enough to take his eyes off her. She watched him walk to the car and get in. Mia sat in the passenger's seat with her face still hidden.

Aliette reached into her purse and grabbed her cell phone. She continued to look outside at Wayne and Mia as she dialed Sinclair's number. Even though they had been fighting, Sinclair was still the only person Aliette felt like she could call when her life was full of too much drama. When Sinclair's answering machine came on, Aliette threw her phone back in her purse, never hanging up. As she watched Wayne and Mia getting ready to pull off, she grabbed her purse and prepared to leave, yelling curses at them through the window. They couldn't hear her, of course, but her cell phone was in her purse, recording everything onto Sinclair's answering machine.

Wayne started his car and Aliette prepared to follow them. She waited a few seconds before she was in her car and right behind them. Wayne drove and she followed him at a safe distance. They drove for about two and a half miles, and Wayne never noticed Aliette's car. They pulled into a condominium complex and parked. Wayne got out and went to open Mia's door. She got out and followed him into the condo.

"Oh, I see. This bastard is playing house with this bitch," Aliette slurred. When she grabbed her bottle, she accidentally pushed the horn. Mia heard it and came to the window. She saw Aliette's car, but by that time, Aliette had thrown herself across the seat so Mia wouldn't see her. She waited about five minutes — what seemed an eternity for her — then she drove slowly in front of the unit, got the address and drove off. When she wasn't so drunk, she would come back and cause some trouble for Wayne and his new ho.

Giving a drunken cry, she cruised, remembering what she considered to be good times with Wayne. Peering into the rearview mirror to make sure no one was following her, she pulled over and finished the bottle of Jack Daniel's then drove herself home, drunk as hell.

When Aliette got in the house, she immediately went into the bedroom. She went to Wayne's closet and smelled his clothes. She was still crying when she picked up the phone to make a call. The room was spinning, and she could hardly hold the phone. Thinking that she had dialed Wayne's cell phone number, she waited for him to answer. She hadn't dialed the entire number, though, so an automated voice announced, "If you would like to make a call, please hang up and try again."

Aliette started talking. "Wayne, you're an asshole. And to that tramp, you dirty bitch, you think you can come into my life and take my man? I don't think so. I'm his lady, and we are getting married, so whatever you think is going on between you two, you just better think again, okay, you nasty bitch? And that baby, well, it better think again too." Her words were so slurred that even if she had really been leaving a message on Wayne's voice mail, he wouldn't have been able to understand half of what she said.

Swaying back and forth, Aliette dropped the phone. The receiver emitted a fast-paced beeping sound. Aliette ignored it and walked over to her makeup table, picked up a lipstick and attempted to put it on. She tried the same with her eyeliner. When she was done, she looked in the mirror and laughed.

"Now this is a picture that could win at an art exhibit."

She held her hands up to her eyes as if she had a camera. At first she moved her finger rapidly as she pretended to photograph her makeup-smeared face. She slowed down as she made herself dizzy, then when she couldn't sit up anymore, she fell off her seat and onto the floor. She remained there for a little while until she was able to crawl to the bed where she lay half on and half off.

It was quarter to seven when Sinclair got out of the shower. Ja'qazz would be there in fifteen minutes, and she still needed to do something with her hair. She wanted to be creative, so she went into the kitchen and found the extra set of chopsticks from the last time he was there. She went back into the bathroom, gathered her hair up onto the top of her head and stuck the chopsticks haphazardly in her hair.

"I like this. I look sexy," she said, "but I don't feel so sexy. I feel like shit, but I'll get through the night, I'm sure."

She dressed in a white T-shirt and linen pants. No shoes, though. Hopefully, Ja would get the hint to suck on her toes.

As promised, Ja'qazz was there at seven on the dot. Very happily, he walked up to the door. Sinclair watched him until his face was right in front of the peephole. She watched as he fixed his clothing and patted his hair. He got his stance correct before he rang her bell. She didn't open the door immediately as she was just checking him out. After making him wait for a few more seconds, she opened the door and acted surprised.

"Hey, baby girl," he purred as he reached for her and gave her a big hug. "Damn, I missed you."

"I missed you too. Come on in."

They went to the couch and sat in total silence, gazing at each other. He leaned over and kissed her on the lips. He didn't slip his tongue in, so she was able to feel his lips cover hers and feel the warmth they delivered.

"Wow. What was that for?"

"Sinclair, I wanted to come over to talk to you about us. We've been seeing each other for just a short time, I know. But all I think about is you. I don't go out as much as I used to, nor do I want to. I wonder what you're doing when you're not around me, and I miss you the minute you say bye. I want to get to know the whole person, not just bits and pieces. I want to know that when I get up in the morning, the plan for that day will be to look into your eyes. I want to know that when I come home, I need to cook for two or three, or however many. I'm ready to settle down, and I would like it to be with you."

"Ja, I don't know what to say. I mean, yes, we've only been seeing each other for a week or so. I really like your company. We have a good time and all, but I don't know if I'm ready for that yet. Look at where you're sitting. You're in the same house I shared with my ex-husband. Do you know why I'm still here? I don't. You would think that when you divorce someone, you let go of everything. But when we divorced, the only thing that was thrown out was Vernon.

"When Al and I were out last night," she went on to explain, "we ran into him. Seeing him again brought back feelings. I don't know just yet if they're good or bad. All I know is that at the end of the night, I came to terms with the fact that he came back into my life for a reason, and I need to know why. I need to face him and get whatever is going on out into the open. How fair is that to you when you have these feelings for me?"

"Don't try to convince yourself that I'm the only one who has feelings here, Sinclair. I see the way you look at me. I feel your love for me when you touch me. You can't deny yourself a true and natural love. Whatever you have to do to close the chapter between you and your ex, go do it. If you come to the conclusion you need to explore possibly getting back together, then do that too. But if you think I'm going to walk away from you just because you're unsure, you're wrong. The reality is you were married to this man. There was something that attracted you to him, and if it's still there, then you need to work that out.

"I'm a grown man. Your being honest with me gives me the opportunity to decide whether I want to remain in this situation, and I'm telling you that I do. I will back off as much as you need me to, and I will be there for you whenever you need to talk about it, or whatever else is on your mind. I want a friendship with you, because if we don't have that, we'll have nothing, no matter how we come at this relationship."

"Oh, Ja." Sinclair sighed. "You promise that no matter what happens we'll still have our friendship? Regardless of whether I end up getting back with Vernon or if I choose not to be in a relationship with anyone, we will still remain friends?"

"I promise. I love you no matter what."

He held her close while they sat on the couch. Her legs were draped over his, and she was rubbing the back of his head. Turning toward her, he looked into her eyes. Her stomach dropped; she was weak for him. He moved closer to her face and their lips barely brushed against each other. In a circular motion, he moved his face to smell her and to feel her breath. She pulled back, got up from his lap, took his hand and led him into the bathroom. She ran a hot, steamy shower.

As all of him stood erect, she slowly undressed him. When she was done, she took his hands and told him to undress her. They got in the shower and let the water run down their bodies. With her back to him and his hands around her waist, she turned just enough for him to lick the back of her ear. She bent forward so that his body cupped hers and he slowly rubbed his penis in the crack of her butt. She bent down more, and he followed her lead until he entered her.

Their warm skin clapped like hands at the end of a scene that was full of intense and erotic sex. His strong hands rubbed her back. She could feel his passion. Sinclair reached under and walked her fingers over his pot of gold. This excited him even more. He turned her head so she could see him. He looked into her eyes, letting her know he was all hers if she wanted him. He stroked her.

Sinclair was in ecstasy. This man was loving her—not fucking her, loving her. He was gentle, yet confident. He was in control of letting her be in control. She gently pulled away and turned to face him.

"You're my angel, Sinclair." He took her face in his hands and kissed her. "I'll wait for you. Whatever you need, I'll give it to you."

He reached over her and grabbed the soap. He lathered up and began to wash her body. Starting from her feet, he rubbed her toes, massaged her calves, softly squeezed her thighs, swiped her vagina just enough, turned her around and massaged her back. Then he rinsed his hands and poured shampoo into them. He rubbed them together then proceeded to wash her hair. When he was done, he rinsed her whole body. Then he got out of the shower and reached for a towel. She turned off the water before she walked into his arms, where he held the towel.

Slowly and softly, he patted her dry and wrapped her hair. He dried himself off with another towel, wrapped it around his waist, grabbed her robe and put it on her. They went into the bedroom where he rubbed rose-scented lotion all over her body. When he was done, he kissed her good night, turned off the light and went into the living room where he slept the entire night.

"Oh, hell yeah," she whispered as she lay in her bed and realized he had just put her there like she was a baby. She fell asleep believing that what she had just seen could only happen once in a lifetime.

Chapter 20
Ms. Mia

Mia rubbed her stomach and Wayne watched while he took a break from writing an article. Their relationship had happened by accident. Wayne was out one night, chilling at Barry's with Grant and Aaron, when he met her. They had just come in and were doing a little bit of cutting up when Mia walked in and took a seat a few tables away from them.

Wayne was joking around with Grant when they noticed her.

"Damn, bro, who the hell is that?" Grant asked.

"I don't know, bro, but watch a brotha and— well, just watch." He made his way over to where Mia sat. She was fine. She stood five-four, about 115 pounds with straight, black hair. Her skin looked like milk with a bit of honey evenly mixed throughout. Mia's skin accentuated her hazel eyes, and she was dressed in the best. As Wayne got up close to her, he thought, *Damn, she looks yummy.*

"Excuse me, miss," he said as he pulled a chair out and sat down, "but I couldn't help but notice you. I'm not going to beat around the bush." *But if you want me to, I will.* "You are fine."

"Ah, thank you," Mia responded shyly.

"You're welcome. Um, are you here alone?"

"Mm-hmm." She nodded.

"Well, you can move over to our table and hang with us if you want."

She looked over at Grant and Aaron. They were arm wrestling for dollars.

"No. Thank you, though. I'll stay here. I wouldn't want to impose."

"Are you sure?"

"Yes, I am. Really."

"Can I chill with you, then?"

"What about your friends? Are you sure they don't need you to. . . " She paused. "...referee them?"

By now, their arm wrestling had turned into a full-fledged wrestling match. There was a small crowd around them, egging them on.

"They'll be okay." Wayne laughed. "Besides, I like it over here better. Are you from around here?"

"Actually, I live in Long Island. I'm here searching for a job because I want to relocate to be closer to my family. I heard about this place and figured I would stop in and see what's happening. It's nice. I like it."

"Let me show you around. You know that they have other floors here. You like R&B or reggae? What about oldies but goodies?"

"Yeah, sure. Let's go," she agreed.

As they walked up to the mid-level, Wayne could hear they were playing his song.

"That's my song," he said. "Come on, let's dance."

That was it. There was an obvious attraction on both parts, and by the end of the night they had exchanged phone numbers. For a while they were talking on the sneak tip, pretending they were just friends. But not long afterward, neither of them could deny their attraction, and they decided to hook up. They got together a few times. Sometimes they used protection and sometimes they didn't, and as a result of their lust for each other, Mia got pregnant.

When she found out she was pregnant, Mia called and told Wayne immediately. She also told him she didn't expect anything from him, but he would still be welcome to see the baby whenever he wanted. She just wanted them to remain friends.

That was good for Wayne. It relieved him to know Mia was going to be cool about it; she wasn't the vindictive type. And since he knew he could rely on Mia to be his friend, he decided it gave him even more reason to tell Aliette the truth and end their engagement. That way when he moved out of Aliette's place, he could share a place with Mia until he found something for himself. They could be friends, and he would be there for the baby when Mia gave birth.

As Wayne sat and looked through a magazine, Mia stood in front of the mirror behind her closet door and looked at her stomach.

"So much for belly rings," she commented as she rubbed her stomach. "In a few months, I won't be able to see my coochie."

"You're a trip, girl," Wayne said as he laughed. "Have you decided on any names for the baby?"

"It's still early yet. But if it's a girl, I think I'm going to name her Chloe. If it's a boy, I don't know."

"Chloe? That's nice. I like it, but don't you think you should have a boy name just in case you have a boy? In case *we* have a boy?"

"I guess I should. I'm not into juniors and seconds and thirds, so it won't be Wayne."

"I'm cool with that."

She smiled at him. He got up, gave her a hug and kissed her on the cheek. He was going to be a father. The circumstances in which it was happening weren't what he had planned, but for some reason, everything felt okay. He was happy with no strings attached. They were two people having a baby together, and they were friends as well, an uncommon combination.

"You don't know how much I appreciate you letting me stay here until my place is ready. When I gave the landlord the down payment, she didn't tell me the water heater was busted and that it needed to be replaced. Now it will be a week or two—or maybe even three—before I move in, and I didn't have the money to put down on another place. Not to mention the patience to look for another place to stay. Thank you, again, so much for your understanding and friendship. Love you, girl."

"Oh Wayne, please, you don't have to thank me. I know you appreciate our relationship. Hey, how did she take it when you told her you were leaving?" Mia asked, referring to Aliette. After all the stories Wayne had told about her and what she had witnessed herself, Mia didn't even like to speak her name.

"Contrary to what I expected, she was really calm until I told her about the baby and that I had an apartment already lined up. It took her a few minutes to respond, but that was the quiet before the storm. She went off for a while, but she also started talking about counseling." He laughed. "We are so far beyond counseling."

"So you feel okay, then?" Mia asked.

"More than okay. I'd given it a lot of thought before I decided to leave her. I knew I had to do something about this mess she called a relationship. When I thought about life without her, I wasn't sad. I was excited. That's when I knew I had to go. Our love was totally false. Shit, I didn't even like her as a person anymore. There was no repairing the relationship."

"Wow, that's pretty intense. And you said she knows about the baby?"

"Yes. I told her."

"Okay, well, did you tell her anything about me?"

"No. She asked who you were, but I told her she didn't need to know. I also told her you were keeping the baby and I was going to make sure you have a healthy and safe pregnancy. I know her. If I would've told her anything about you, there would definitely be some drama. But don't worry. I have it under control."

"I hope so because I just don't want to have to deal with anybody's issues. I need to know from you that she won't know anything about me, at least not yet. I don't want to have to Tae-Bo her ass."

They both laughed. Mia went to bed and Wayne finished reading the magazine. When his phone rang, he looked at the caller ID. He saw it was coming from Aliette's house, so he let it go to his voice mail. He gave it time to register then he checked his message.

"Wayne, the locks are going to be changed first thing tomorrow." Aliette's voice sounded cold. "You'll need to call in advance and ask me when you can come and get your things. And don't even try bringing that bitch back over here. I *will* cut up. Bye. Punk."

"She's got issues," Wayne said to himself. "I swear, I'm so glad I'm not marrying her."

He already knew he was going to have a problem when he went there to get his things, and this call just made him even more certain. He decided he would just wait until he had his own place to clean out his things. This way, if she decided to have him followed, he wouldn't be followed to Mia's place.

When he finished reading, it was late. He got something to drink and went into the guestroom where he slept.

The next morning while Sinclair was drinking her orange juice, she noticed her message light was blinking. She pressed play, and listened to the very distorted and nasty message Aliette had inadvertently left. Sinclair stared at the answering machine in amazement. She went over to wake Ja'qazz so he could listen because she couldn't believe what she had heard.

"Listen to her. She was drunk off her ass. Who was she calling? She must have misdialed or something. We had a fight, yeah, but I don't think she would call and leave this type of message."

"I don't know, Sin. Your girl sounds like she fell off her rocker. What's up with her? Why is she bugging? And y'all had a fight about what?"

"Wayne broke off the engagement, and she was tripping for real. When we were at the club the other night, I lost it on her. We had a downright fistfight. I ended up leaving her there."

"You want to talk about it?"

Sinclair stared into space, slowly shaking her head.

"I'm here if you need me, Sin."

"I know, Ja."

She gave Ja a kiss and told him to stay as long as he wanted. She had to go take care of something.

Chapter 21
T.B.O. aka "The Busted One"

Sinclair was on her way to Aliette's house, thinking about the crazy message that had been left on her machine. Aliette must have dialed the number by accident, Sinclair thought. Her voice was kind of crazy, though, kind of muffled. Who knew what she was talking about? Well, Sinclair was determined to find out.

As Sinclair went to Aliette's door to knock, she noticed it wasn't closed all the way. It was very unlikely Aliette would leave the door cracked on purpose. A bit hesitant, Sinclair pushed the door open and stuck her head in. She called out Aliette's name then stepped inside. She looked around her place; it was a mess. Nothing was in its usual place. For sure, this wasn't Aliette's way of housekeeping. Aliette was one of the neatest and cleanest people Sinclair knew.

Sinclair headed to the bedroom, where she saw Aliette sprawled on the bed, still in her clothes from the day before.

"Why am I here?" Sinclair asked herself aloud.

The smell of liquor hung in the air. The phone was off the hook, and Aliette's makeup dresser was a disaster. Sinclair approached Aliette and rolled her over. She looked a hot mess. Makeup was all over her face and on her bed linen.

What the hell? Sinclair thought. "Aliette," Sinclair called out as she shook her in an attempt to wake her. After several tries, she grabbed and hung up the phone, went into the kitchen and put on some coffee. On her way there, she yelled out to Aliette.

"Wake up, Aliette. We got some unfinished business. I don't appreciate that message you left on my machine."

I should leave her ass there, she thought as she straightened up the kitchen a little. She went back into the bedroom and as hard as it was, she undressed Aliette and dragged her into the bathroom. She started the water and made it as cold as possible. *I'll wake that wench up.*

"Okay, girl, we're gonna get you into this tub because we can't have you looking like this. I don't know what's going on with you, and I don't know why I'm helping your simple ass after all the mess we've been through, but it's gonna be okay. Come on. Help me out. You are heavy as hell."

Aliette could hear Sinclair from the minute she came in, but she just couldn't get it together enough to respond.

Get out, Sinclair. You aren't my friend, so don't bother fronting anymore, Aliette thought as she went in and out of consciousness.

But Sinclair wasn't going away. Aliette listened to Sinclair's footsteps as she paced around the room, straightening out the mess and preparing the bathroom for Aliette's shower. Aliette realized Sinclair was there for real, and she knew Sinclair would be the friend she needed her to be, regardless of what they were going through. Still, her foolish pride wouldn't let her accept Sinclair's help without a fight.

"Get off me!" Aliette screamed as Sinclair tried to lift her off the floor into the tub.

"And then what, Aliette? It's not like anyone else is gonna come and help your ass," Sinclair countered. "Trust me, I wish I wasn't the one to find you here, and don't ask me where I'm getting the strength to help you out of your drunken stupor."

Sinclair tried to lift Aliette's leg into the bathtub as the rest of Aliette's body fell limp. Aliette's eyes remained closed because she knew if she opened them, the tears that had welled up throughout the night would race down her cheeks.

Sinclair finally got her in the tub, went back into the kitchen, poured a cup of coffee and took her time walking back to the bathroom. She didn't want to risk Aliette waking up and seeing her cry.

Never in her wildest dreams had Sinclair thought she would come to feel responsible for Aliette, especially with the unfortunate way their lives had become intertwined through Vernon, all the secrets they had kept from each other, and the way things had been between them these last few days. Deep down inside, though, Sinclair felt sorry for Aliette. Her life was really empty, without love and companionship. Aliette was clearly full of issues that were calling the shots in her life. Sinclair and Aliette were friends by accident, but friends nonetheless, and Sinclair couldn't let her friend fall without being there to pick her up.

"Aliette, you better thank my momma for this one," Sinclair announced as she entered the bathroom.

Aliette appeared to still be passed out, so Sinclair got undressed and got in the tub with her. She sat behind Aliette with her legs around her waist and Aliette lay against her chest. Sinclair tilted Aliette's head so she could sip on the coffee without choking. She was able to get her to drink about a quarter of it, then Sinclair just sat there with Aliette, freezing. After about twenty minutes of waiting, Aliette finally came to.

"Why are we in a cold-ass tub? And you better have on your underwear. Boobs all in my face and shit."

"I know you're not talking about me with your breath smelling like hot garbage. I don't even know why I'm in this cold-ass tub tryin'a get you together. If my mother hadn't taught me any better, you'd still be passed out in your bed. Now that you're up, let's get out. I'm freezing," Sinclair said.

They got up one at a time, Aliette first, then Sinclair. Each grabbed a towel out of the hall closet and retreated to Aliette's bedroom. Sinclair silently pulled the sheets off the bed while Aliette lingered around. Sinclair took the sheets into the laundry room. Aliette was embarrassed by the way she looked, and followed Sinclair like a child who needed to know what to do next.

"So, Aliette," Sinclair said, "I got a foul message on my machine this morning. It's your voice, muffled like it was somewhat distant from the receiver. Our argument—or whatever you want to call it — wasn't all like that. So, I guess I'm just wondering who that message was meant for."

"Sin, I was drunk as hell. I couldn't even tell you. Maybe I was thinking out loud or something."

"Well, damn, Al, those were some pretty foul thoughts. Who were you trying to call? Do you have something else you need to say to me?"

"I don't remember making a phone call from the house, Sinclair. The last call I remember making was when I was trying to call you from my cell phone, and I was in the car when I did that. I honestly don't remember, so please don't start tripping again."

"I'm telling you that it was your voice, and you left the message on my machine. You don't remember? What did you have to drink? Come to think of it, you have been sipping a lot. I hope you have it under control."

Sinclair looked at the bare mattress. "Look at these stains. You're gonna need to get the sheets and comforter professionally treated."

"Look, Sinclair, take your advice and your negative comments and see your way out," Aliette told her. "I've had enough of your judgmental attitude, always thinking you're better than everybody.

"Yes, I fucked your husband. You knew this when you met me. But you couldn't let it go. You had to try to get revenge on me. But what have you accomplished? You're just as miserable today as you were the day I saw you in the park. You've probably been crying the last twenty-four hours just like you were that day. So really, was it worth it? Do you feel any better?"

"No, Aliette, I don't. Well, I did, but now I'm angry."

"Angry at what, Sinclair?"

"Angry because you were able to move on with your vacant life totally unconcerned about how your actions affected anyone, and I had to figure out a way to somehow deal with my feelings."

"You could've done that nine months ago, Sinclair. You didn't have to put on this long and drawn-out charade, acting like we were friends. A real woman would've dealt with it right then and there. And if your life was about anything, you wouldn't have needed to do all of that. Are you sure yours wasn't as vacant as you say mine is?"

Sinclair was silent.

"I didn't hear you," Aliette said.

"You don't know what it is to love someone and lose —"

"The hell I don't, Sinclair. Just because I cheated on Wayne doesn't mean I didn't love him. I loved him. I just didn't love myself. And look at me now. I'm ass out."

"What do we do now, Aliette?"

"Hell, you were the one calling plays on the down low. What do you want to do? And let me say this, if you plan on continuing to act like we're friends or whatever, you can roll. Just be on your way, because I got enough to deal with without having to worry about you having it out for me." Aliette turned to walk out of the room.

"Wait, Aliette." Sinclair sounded like she was pleading.

Aliette stopped in her tracks and stood with her back to Sinclair. *Thank you, God,* she silently prayed.

"Let's go and get some breakfast and talk. My treat," Sinclair said. "We really just need to talk."

"Okay. I'm cool with that." Aliette tried not to reveal just how happy she was that there was still hope for their friendship.

While Sinclair was putting her clothes back on, Aliette grabbed a pair of jeans and a T-shirt, brushed her teeth and pulled her hair back into a ponytail. Sinclair, who was dressed in slacks and a blazer, looked at Aliette like she was crazy.

"Excuse me. Since when do we go out looking all busted up and shit? You never dressed like that, even on a bad day. You look—well, let's just go," she said, sucking her teeth.

There was no response from Aliette. She just grabbed her purse, pulled out her black glasses and headed for the door. Sinclair followed her out.

They decided to go to a little diner about two blocks away. The day was dewy, and it looked like it was going to rain. Sinclair looked over at Aliette, who felt her staring and looked back at her.

"Talk to me, Aliette. No more hiding our feelings."

"I don't know, Sinclair," Aliette responded.

"Aliette, yesterday we talked okay, argued about you and Vernon. I really want you to know that I'm gonna try really hard to get over this as far as you and I are concerned. So please, you need to open up and talk to me. I can't make amends by myself."

"Sinclair, I really feel bad about sleeping with your husband. I'm guilty and I'm sorry, but that's all I can say."

"Don't feel guilty now. You didn't feel guilty then. Neither you nor Vernon can ever take away the pain and rejection I felt back then. An apology is useless. Don't say it now just because you think it would make me feel better. What's done is done."

"I know, Sinclair, but — "

"Aliette, let's agree to move on and put this shit behind us. The only thing I want from you now is for you to take me to him. I know you know where he's staying. He told you at the club. Remember?"

"Can you stop talking so loud? I remember."

"Set it up then, okay?"

"Why? If you're trying to get over it, then why do you want to talk to him? Don't you think you're opening yourself up to more problems?"

"Problems? What kind of problems, and why do you care if I talk to him again or not?"

"I'm just saying . . . I can set it up, but you already told me how you feel about it. I don't want you to come back to me with any drama, especially since we're agreeing to put it behind us."

"Okay, I feel you on that, but this isn't about you. It's about Vernon and me. I need closure for myself. Just do it. Please."

"Alright, girl," Aliette agreed then changed the subject. "I'm hungry for something salty."

Aliette had ordered a pork roll, an egg-and-cheese sandwich, a side of fried potatoes and a side of bacon. Sinclair ordered bacon, lettuce and tomato on whole-wheat toast. While their food was being prepared, Sinclair went to the ladies' room. As Aliette sat there waiting, she looked around the diner.

Pretty nice place, she thought, *kind of like a hotel lounge.* Then she remembered she was supposed to meet Vernon at nine o'clock the night before. She reached for her phone and called him.

"Good morning. The Spot Light, it's on you. How may I direct your call?"

"Vernon Gushon's room, please."

"Yes, one moment please," the lady said.

"Hello."

"Vernon, it's me. I completely forgot about last night. Sorry. What are your plans for the day?"

"I was going to try to get an early flight back to Wheeling, but I really think we need to talk. How soon can you come over?"

"I'm eating breakfast right now, but I can come when I'm through," she said, biting her lip.

"That's cool. I'll be here. I'll give a heads-up to the front desk to send you right up."

"See you then."

She hung up the phone. *Well,* she thought, *Sinclair wanted me to set it up, so I just did.*

Sinclair returned to their table and Aliette advised her they would be going to see Vernon after they ate. Sinclair couldn't have been happier. As they were leaving the diner, they ran into Grant and Eddie, two of Wayne's boys. Taken a bit off guard, Sinclair spoke out of habit, and Aliette spoke because she didn't know what else to do. In her heart, she felt angry with them because she thought they knew Wayne was leaving her. She wasn't that close to them, but they had come to her house many times and eaten her food. Somehow, she felt betrayed now.

"Yeah, what's up," she said with a slight nod. She didn't wait for an answer; she just continued out the door.

"What's up with her, Sinclair?" Eddie asked.

"Come on, now. Don't act like you don't know Wayne broke off their engagement."

"Oh, yo, you lying," Grant said. "I knew he was tired of her shit and wanted to scare her into acting right, but he never told us he was gonna break it off. Well, I guess he was more fed up than he let on. You know, he gave her everything she needed and anything she wanted."

"Tell me the truth. Did you guys know?" Sinclair asked.

"No. Brothas don't talk all like that," Eddie responded

"So you had no idea?" Sinclair pushed for more information.

"Look, all I know is that he met some chick, and they basically hooked up every now and then."

"What chick?"

"What was her name, Grant? Mia, Mya or something like that?" Eddie asked.

"It's Mia," Grant confirmed

"Mia who?" Sinclair asked.

"Mia Moore. Yeah, that's it. We don't know too much about her because he never brought her around us. We preferred it that way since we knew Aliette and didn't feel too cool about it. So when you get a chance, let her know that. She seems to have the ass with us, and I gather that's why."

"Y'all take it easy. See you around," Sinclair said and walked out of the door.

When she got in the car, she looked at Aliette, who was fuming. Sinclair wasn't concerned about that, though. She wanted to get to Vernon.

"Okay, Aliette, tell me where The Spot Light is so that I can get to Vernon and have the spotlight on me."

Chapter 22
Roundtable #1

There was a knock at the door as Vernon got out of the shower. He threw on a pair of boxers and a shirt, which he didn't bother to button, then he opened the door. Aliette stood in the doorway, blocking his view of Sinclair. Vernon told her to come in and proceeded to shut the door, but a foot at the bottom of the door stopped it from closing. He peeked around and saw Sinclair was standing there with her arms folded on her chest.

"Can I come in, too, or should I go and get a camera crew?" He remained silent, but waved a hand, indicating she could come in. She did. Aliette was real nervous now, because if anything went down, there was nowhere to run.

Vernon, equally as nervous, stood there like the imbecile he was. Sinclair took a seat at the table. She invited them both to sit down and reassured them there would be no cursing or fighting and carrying on.

She started the conversation by saying, "Vernon, the last time you and I were together in the same room, you were trying to explain your way out of one of your infamous lies. I didn't allow you to say a word. You're probably wondering why I'm here, right? I wanted to give you a chance to finally say your peace, for my own edification and to laugh a little. So, any time you're ready . . .".

"Sin," Vernon said pleadingly, "I was stupid and immature. I wanted to have my cake and eat it too. I wasn't man enough to accept you as you were, so I searched elsewhere to meet sexual desires for two reasons. First, I was afraid of rejection from you if I kept on wanting it, and second, I was just dumb."

"So basically you were being selfish," Sinclair said. "Never mind the committed and reverent wife you had at home. You had to go and get it—" she paused and looked at Aliette— "elsewhere. Vernon, you sound like you've been rehearsing this apology for months. I ain't looking for that. You need to know that on a day that I was crying my eyes out, feeling worthless, Aliette came into my life and captured all that. By the way, where is my picture?" she asked Aliette. "From that point on, I had started putting my life and emotions back together, and it was fueled by a plan to get the woman who ruined my marriage. Every day, I looked for the chance to get Aliette back. I had a few successful attempts, and I was getting myself back on track, or so I thought. But then the chances kept coming and coming. I tasted the revenge; I wanted it so bad. She was getting hers, but I still wasn't feeling any better inside. We even fought. Can you believe that?"

"Sinclair," Vernon said as he walked toward her. Aliette moved out of the way.

"Back it up, brotha. I'm not done. When we saw you at the lounge, I realized the person I needed to deal with was you. You were the one who was committed to me, and you said 'I do' to me. Feelings that I didn't know I was capable of surfaced again when I saw you, and they confused me. They actually had me thinking that I still might love your goofy ass.

"Well, I'm glad to say that seeing you today has voided that thought for me. The only thing I feel right now is closure. You, Aliette and I are here together, and I want both of you to know that I'm done with this situation. For good. Now, if only the other woman were here. Hell, who knows what I would be feeling?

"See, Vernon, I want to thank you for giving me this lesson. Thank you for teaching me what I don't want in a man, and thank you for letting me learn my self-worth through your actions."

"Aliette, if I had a choice back then, I wouldn't have wanted to ever see you face-to-face. For whatever reason, it worked out differently for you and me. Again, I accept it.

"I've grown through this whole situation, and I believe I came into your life to teach you self-worth, to walk beside you through your troubles and shit, and I hope you see that you, too, have got some serious soul searching to do."

"Excuse me?" Aliette said with an attitude.

"Ahem." Sinclair cleared her throat. "Hold it right there. Women who sleep with other women's husbands or men and cheat on their man have issues. They—you, Aliette—lack self-esteem and self-worth."

"Oh, please, Sinclair," Vernon began, but Sinclair interrupted him.

"So like I was saying, this isn't a sad moment. Let's all be happy that no one has to hide anymore, feel shame or embarrassment. It's all out in the open now. I know, I know, once again I have taken over the speech, but rest assured, I shall say no more about it. This situation in my life is past. Vernon, peace, brother. Aliette, I'll be downstairs. I gather you guys have some things you want to discuss, and by all means, take your time."

She grabbed her purse and walked out the room with her head held high and a tight strut. Vernon, with his chin chilling on the floor again, watched her as she left. Aliette couldn't help but chuckle to herself.

"Vernon, I really don't know what to say to you right now. I mean, we did what we did, she knows, and it's now the past."

"Al, you two are friends, best friends?" Vernon still couldn't believe it.

"I have to say that she's my best friend — hell, my only friend. I'm not too sure if I'm hers, but I'm thankful for the part she has played and continues to play in my life. I have to admit, I wouldn't be able to handle this if I were in her shoes. You lost a good woman, and friend, I might add. I think I need to go. Take care, Vernon, and I hope you find happiness someday. Bye."

Aliette left feeling lifted of a burden that she didn't know she carried until Sinclair put everything on the table. She could breathe easy and not walk on eggshells anymore.

"Whew, I need a drink," she said as she walked to the elevator. On her way down, she thought about Wayne. She still loved him dearly and was still determined to fight for him.

The bar was empty with the exception of Sinclair.

"What are you drinking?" Aliette asked as she approached Sinclair.

"Kendall Jackson, like you needed to ask, and no, it's not past twelve o'clock. I feel the need to celebrate my new life. I'm about to make some major changes."

"Really? Like what, Sinclair?"

Sinclair looked Aliette in her eyes. "Aliette, I'm not gonna lie to you. I want to fuck you up right now. I really do. But I'm satisfied with things as they are. You got back what you dished out, and I don't have to go to jail behind kicking your ass. Make no mistake about it, we have a long way to go before we will be calling ourselves friends."

"I understand, Sinclair. So, what are you gonna do now?" Aliette asked.

"Get rid of anything from my past that could breed negativity. You can come for the ride, but only if you're on a positive note. I'm not dealing with nobody who can't help me become a better person 'cause if they ain't helping me, they're only hurting me. And that includes yo' ass."

"Bartender, can I get a Jack and ginger please?"

They toasted again. "To life and the obstacles that I keep jumping over while living it," Sinclair said.

"To the truth: May it set you free and lift your heavy heart." They clinked glasses and threw their drinks down.

While they sat at the bar, Vernon came out of the elevator with his bags in his hand. He felt them watching him, but his pride was so bruised he couldn't lift his head up to face them. He jumped into a waiting taxi and left.

"Aliette, I need to go to work. I didn't call in, and I have a lot of things I need to do. I'll drop you back off to your house."

"Cool with me."

When Sinclair walked into the office, her boss was waiting for her. He silently pointed her in the direction of his office. She walked casually and tried to reach into her pocket for a mint, hoping to mask the smell of liquor on her breath. She took a seat and waited for him to come in. Her first thought was that she was in trouble, but when he came in smiling, that changed her thoughts immediately.

"Sinclair, you have been here some years now. Your learning and sales skills are commendable, and I wanted to talk to you about that. Recently, you brought in an account — Barry's, I believe. Where did you get that lead from?"

"Well, actually, the gentleman who I was doing this for is a friend. He gave me some ideas, and I just ran with it in the hopes that it would come out good. I did it as a one-time deal, you know, for a friend."

"Not exactly, Sinclair. In fact, it came out so well that we're broadening our spectrum and customer base, and we want you to lead the project. Now, that would include sales and marketing and launching a search for employees, and of course you need to come up with a budget so that we can get you going." He didn't even wait for a response from Sinclair. He could tell by her smile that she was thrilled. "Congratulations, you are now the manager of New Accounts and Marketing," he stated as he got up to shake her hand.

"Thank you so much. I'm so shocked."

"Don't be. We have been a small family-owned company for a long time. We appreciate all you have done for us. In addition, I won't be spending as much time in the office, so spread your wings and let your ideas soar. Here are the keys to the building. We are buying the one next to us, so hire as you see fit."

He walked out of his office and closed the door. She just sat there, speechless.

A moment later he returned to say, "Oh, and here are the keys to this office. It's yours now. Where are your old keys? I'll be taking that office to hold a desk and a chair for when I do decide to come in," he teased with a huge smile on his face. "And take the rest of the day off after you look in that top drawer and get your check. It's forty percent of your new salary. I'm sure you can do the math."

She tossed the keys and showed all of her teeth. *Wow,* she thought, *I'm basically running this place. Only if Ma could see me now.*

She reached for the phone and called Ja'qazz. The machine came on. She called his name and told him to answer, but he didn't, so she figured she would tell him the good news later. On her way out of the office, she realized as her old, negative feelings were being released, she felt refreshed and wide open. It was like releasing all that pent up-pain had left room for the wonderful things that seemed to be getting ready to happen in her life. Smiling, she hopped in her car and took off.

Chapter 23
The Angry Ex

Her bar was stocked and Aliette reached for what had become her new drink, Jack Daniel's and ginger ale. Slowly mixing it with her index finger, she sat on the couch to think about her next step. The phone rang and broke her concentration.

"Aliette, Wayne here. I was wondering if now would be a good time to come over and sort through the things in my office."

"Sort? Aren't you taking all your shit?"

"Yes, I am, but right now I just need some specific papers, and besides, my place isn't ready yet."

"I thought you had your place and everything already figured out. If it isn't ready, where are you staying?" She tried to keep the attitude out of her voice.

"With a friend. What does this have to do with anything? Can I come or not?"

"I don't care. Come on."

"Give me an hour." They both hung up without saying good-bye. Aliette remained on the couch long enough to copy the number off the caller ID. She guessed he had probably called from Mia's. She jumped up, took a big gulp of her drink and went into her bedroom.

What a mess. I'll clean it later, she thought. She went into the bedroom and put on what she thought was sexy: a long, gray Willi Wear skirt and a white Willi Wear wrap shirt. Her toes weren't manicured, but she remained barefoot anyway. Then she went into the bathroom and brushed her teeth.

Looking closely in the mirror, she could see that her skin was dry and blotchy and her eyes had bags. She blamed it on the lack of good sleep she was missing. She washed her face and pulled her hair up, hoping she didn't really look as bad as she felt.

"There, he always liked when I put on casual clothes." She went into the closet and pulled out her camera and tripod. She took them into the office and set up, laying a few pieces of clothing over it to hide the timer light. She set it for ninety minutes and five shots. By the time they talked a bit, the timer would be ready to go off.

She heard a door close, then another, and went to the window, thinking it would be Wayne. It was Grant and Eddie.

"Damn, what the hell are Frick and Frack doing here? They never come over without Wayne. Today would be the day. What idiots," she whispered. Before they could get to the door, she opened it and met them outside.

"Hello, and what is it that I can do for you?"

"Aliette, we just wanted to come over and talk to you. You looked real mad when we saw you a little while ago, and we wanted you to know that we honestly didn't know about Mia and Wayne. He's our boy, yeah, but we were friends with you too. We don't want any bad blood or hard feelings."

"Mia, huh?" Aliette said as she rolled her eyes. "Well, I know about her, and it's cool. Now, I have some things to do. If that's all, peace."

"Aliette, you be cool now," Eddie said as he reached for her hand.

"Yeah, we'll be coming around to check up on you, if that's okay," Grant added.

"Thanks, but no thanks. See ya." Aliette turned back to her door without waiting for them to say good-bye.

Eddie looked at Grant and shrugged. They walked back to the car just as Wayne was pulling up.

"Yo, what are you guys doing here?" Wayne asked with surprise.

"Bro, we just came by to talk to Aliette. Let her know we were still cool. Why didn't you tell us you and ole girl, you know, was banging on a regular?" Eddie asked Wayne.

"So that you can say you really didn't know. Besides, that's my business."

"Right, right," Grant replied with an *I ain't mad at ya* look.

They joked around a bit then Grant and Eddie left. Wayne saw Aliette in the doorway and slowly approached her. *Please don't let her trip*, he thought. *I just wanna get my papers and leave.*

Aliette stood at the door, holding it open for him. As he walked in, he started to lean over and give her a kiss out of habit. He caught himself and pulled back. Then he took a few steps out of the doorway and waited for her to give him permission to come in.

"Oh, now I have to formally tell you to come in?" she said in a voice that tried to mask her true emotions.

"You know, I didn't just want to walk in," he answered meekly, trying to keep the peace.

She threw her head back as an indication to him that it was okay, and he went in. A little curious why the place looked disheveled, he asked, "Did we have a party or something and forget to clean up?"

Aliette wasn't in a joking mood. She ignored his question and offered him something to drink.

"I don't know about all that. I just came for a few of my things."

"Wayne, a drink isn't going to hurt you, but be anal if you want to."

"If you have a beer, I'll take that," he said reluctantly. He hoped the beer would help him relax a bit.

"Sure do," Aliette said as she went to get the beer. Wayne went into the office. While he was pushing a few papers around, she came in and looked at the timer. It was set to start shooting photos in thirty minutes. *Perfect*, she thought. She could make small talk, then put the moves on him.

"Wayne, I just wanted you to know that I've had time to think about what happened, and I see why you wouldn't want to be with me. There are things about me that I need to work on, and I intend to do that. Unfortunately, it took you leaving for me to realize that everybody doesn't live to please me. My selfishness is a turnoff, and I invalidated your feelings. I apologize and hope that we can at least remain friends. We have some history, you know, and all of our times weren't bad."

"I hear you, Al. I wish we could be friends, too, but you know how that can go. Most of the time, people need to be away from each other for a while, and I think that's what we need. I know you're hurting because you're not used to people putting their foot down with you, but I was just being honest with you. You deserve someone who loves you for you." He turned his attention back to the papers on his desk. "I'll just be a minute. You don't have to sit with me."

"No, I don't mind, really." She had to keep him talking if her plan was going to work. "In fact, I was wondering what was going on with your place. Why isn't it ready?"

Wayne looked at her with skepticism. "Apparently, they had to replace the hot water heater, and that'll take a few days. In the meantime, I'm staying with a friend."

Now on her second strong drink, Aliette's adrenaline was flowing. She kept it cool until she got the nerve to approach him.

"So, are you saying you don't miss me?" she asked coyly.

"It's not that I don't miss you, Aliette. But what looks good to you isn't always good *for* you, and you and I aren't a good mix right now. Maybe when you get it together and do some work on you we can revisit our situation, but for now, I'm out."

That was it. He opened the door for her to give him something to hold on to, something for him to think about while he lay in his bed at night. She walked behind him, put her arms around his waist and slowly moved her hands over his penis. Lightly touching it, not too hard or too soft, she turned him around. She kissed him slowly and lovingly.

"Can I just touch you one last time, Wayne?"

"No, Aliette," he responded. He hated the fact that she still felt good. He didn't push her away.

She watched him respond to her and knew his absence was only a temporary thing.

"Tell me, Wayne, do you really think you can live without smelling me, tasting me, hearing me call your name?"

He moaned, "Nooo . . . I mean, yeah. Please stop."

I still got him, she thought, *and this Mia girl will know that.*

She heard the beeping of the camera, announcing that she had only ten seconds until showtime. Moaning loudly so that Wayne wouldn't notice the camera's faint beeping, she quickly lowered herself to unzip his pants and went to work on his penis.

Click.

"You like my hot lips on it, huh, Wayne?"

"Yeeeaah . . . I mean no. Damn it, Aliette, don't," he protested weakly.

Click.

She slid up and down his shaft, slightly pulling as she came off the head of his penis.

Click.

In a swirl of motion, she pumped and sucked, pumped and sucked, until he delivered the hot, sticky brotha butter all over her lips.

Click.

Aliette watched him the entire time and when she heard the fifth click, she looked directly in the camera and winked.

This is for you, Mia, she thought. Then she got up and said, "Oh my gosh, Wayne, I'm so embarrassed. I shouldn't have." She ran out of the room, grinning.

Wayne didn't follow her. He put his dick, still dripping, back in his pants, got his papers and left.

Aliette came back into the living room and watched Wayne get into his car and pull off. Immediately she took the film out, grabbed her purse and went to a one-hour photo store to get it processed. While she waited, she went to the card section.

"Hmm, let's see. Would this be a time for a sympathy card or a thank-you card, a card of encouragement or a card of wishing well? Here we go."

She picked up a card with a woman crying as she read a letter. The card was blank inside. When Aliette was done paying for the card, she went to the liquor store across the street and grabbed two miniature bottles of Jack Daniel's and a loose beer. As Aliette exited the liquor store, she downed the two shots. With a brown bag around her beer, she went to her car and sipped as she waited. When the hour was up, she went back into the photo store and paid for the pictures, ignoring the strange looks she was getting from the man who had developed the film.

She got into her car and went home. On her bed, she sat with the pictures spread out in front of her while she thought about what to write on the card. Always good with words, it came rather easy for her. Simple and sweet was always best.

> *Dear Ms. Mom-to-be,*
> *Here's a midnight snack to you from me.*

"No need to sign it. I'm sure she'll figure out who sent it," she said out loud. As tired as she was, she found the strength to make another drink, take a shower and drive herself to Mia's house.

It was dark, and she figured they would be asleep. Aliette parked her car around the corner and walked up to the house. She waited awhile, looking for any sign of movement in the house, then she slowly walked up to the door and went to drop the card through the mail slot.

Suddenly, the front lights came on, and to her surprise, Mia opened the door. Her feet, neatly manicured, accentuated shapely calves, toned thighs, tiny boobs and a glowing face. Mia stood there for a minute looking at how foolish and childish Aliette appeared. Mia's eyes were full of shock while Aliette's were full of shame.

Mia grabbed the envelope and opened it, examining five pictures of Aliette and Wayne. After laughing hysterically, Mia felt really obligated to tell Aliette a few things.

"Not for nothing, Aliette, but why are you giving me these pictures and putting your business out in the street?"

"You think you got my man?" Aliette slurred. "See, he still lets me suck his dick." She pointed to her pussy.

"For your information, doll, Wayne and I aren't together. And neither are you two."

"Don't judge me, bitch. You don't know me."

"You're right. And you don't know me. You came to my place trying to start a whole bunch of mess."

"You started it, Mia, when you got with my man." Aliette was pounding on her chest with a balled fist.

"I'm not doing this with you," Mia said, sounding almost bored. "Wayne and I are just two people who had sex and are having a baby. Get over it."

By this time, Aliette was sitting on the porch with her face in her hands. Mia was standing beside her. Trying not to get too heated, Mia gracefully gave her a little bit more advice.

"If you plan to continue to neglect Wayne, or any man in the future, you can rest assured they will seek affection elsewhere. He'll go out more and make excuses why he doesn't want to be around you." Mia was counting on her fingers.

Aliette turned to Mia and shouted at her. "No! The problem is women like you who have no respect for women like me and push up on our men even after they tell you they're with someone."

"You created your own misery. Your constant bitching and holding out on the sex basically gave him permission to cheat. Withholding sex from a man will eventually leave you at home, sitting by the phone, running to the bathroom because you have diarrhea from anxiety."

"How could you be with a man knowing he was engaged to be married, Mia?"

"You watch too much Lifetime," Mia told Aliette then walked to the house. Before she closed the door, Mia felt the need to say one more thing.

"You're not the first to be left, Aliette, and you won't be the last. So take my advice and get it together because you look like shit."

What could Aliette say? What happened to her was karma, as she had done the same thing to Sinclair. No, she didn't know about Sinclair at the time, but she did see the ring on Vernon's finger. Aliette got up, got in her car and drove off.

Mia stood watching in the window, shaking her head. "I hope she's gonna be alright."

Chapter 24
Moving Right Along

When Sinclair left that morning, Ja'qazz was knocked out. By the time she came back home, he was waiting for her, and her place was sparkling like he'd just had Merry Maids in there.

"Oh, alright, you can clean too," she teased as she walked over to him.

"Sure can. I could be your everything man."

She dropped her purse on the couch, walked over to him and gave him a big kiss. Then, pulling him with her, she headed to the couch and asked him to have a seat.

"I got some good news, baby. I've just been promoted to manager of New Accounts and Marketing at my job. My boss gave me carte blanche to hire and renovate as needed. We're expanding our print jobs to business, commercial and personal printing. In other words, we'll be printing anything for anybody." She stood there with her hands clasped together, smiling from ear to ear.

"Baby, that's great. You've worked very hard for them, and they obviously appreciate you. Congratulations. So what's next?"

"I don't know. I mean, I know my job, but I don't have the faintest idea about hiring, renovating and all that stuff. This all happened so fast. I'm still getting used to the notion that I'm now my own boss.

"My life is finally going the way I've always dreamed. I've lifted a lot off my heart and mind, and I'm convinced that when you have a positive air about you, positive things happen. But that's not it. I want a new life, new things, new everything, if I'm gonna be totally self-renovated."

She got up and walked around the room.

"Look, like I said before, I got a lot of things to change. Oh, and you need to know that I went to speak to Vernon."

A look of uncertainty came over Ja's face.

"Not to worry," she reassured him. "I just needed closure. I didn't want to venture into anything serious with you until I knew in my heart that I felt nothing for him. I took Aliette with me, because she was one of the reasons why we broke up."

"She was?" he asked in amazement. That Aliette was something else.

"Yes," Sinclair explained. "He had a threesome when we were married, and she was one of the girls. How we became friends—well, we'll talk about that another time.

"Ja'qazz, I'm not saying that I see us married in the future or anything. Hell, it's only been a couple of weeks, but I'm willing to take this relationship day by day and see what happens. You must know, however, that the dishonesty I dismissed in my past won't be tolerated from this point forward, from you or anyone else. I don't lie to you, and you will not lie to me. I don't believe in keeping tabs on you, and you should not keep them on me. If you tell me something, I'm going to believe you, but the first time I feel that you've deceived me, we will have to take several steps back and re-evaluate our situation to see if it's something we both want. My days of being the receiver of foul treatment are over. All I want is someone to love me for me, to have my back, not my neck, someone to be my friend first and my lover and companion next.

"So, I mean, take some time. Don't feel obligated to submit to my demands at this very moment. You have a say in what you want, and you really need to think about if I'm what you want.

"Last but not least, I'm selling this place. Tomorrow, I'll find a real estate agent and get it on the market. Everything with the exception of my personal items will stay. There." She let out a huge sigh and a laugh that tickled Ja. Suddenly, he jumped up and embraced her. He looked into her eyes, and he knew that he didn't need time to think about anything. She was exactly what he wanted and needed. Now that she had put everything in the open, he figured he should too.

"Sinclair, now it's your turn to have a seat. I know in the beginning I tried the cowardly way to get to know you, by asking Aliette to hook us up rather than coming to you myself. I apologize again, and I promise to be as honest and up front with you as possible.

"I've also been thinking about my life, and I want to make some changes. My intentions were to do some investing and take a little time off to relax, and I still might do the relaxing part. But, now that you mention your new job and what you're about to do, let me help you. Let me back the company financially and get you started on your project."

"Back them financially? Like you got that kind of money," Sinclair teased.

"Sweetheart, I came from money." He displayed a proud grin as he revealed this fact to Sinclair. She looked totally dumbfounded by the news, so he explained. "My parents bought real estate as I was growing up, and a few properties have been paid off. Some were transferred to me. I own two bed-and-breakfasts in Ocean City, Maryland, and they both do very well. Twice a month, a deposit is made into my account that gives me more than enough to live on. I only worked at Barry's to keep myself busy.

"Now that I'm gonna take some time off from Barry's, I'll go down to Maryland two or three times a year to do any fixing up I have to do, visit my parents and younger brothers, and that's it."

"Why are you just now telling me this?" Sinclair wanted to know.

"We're being honest, right?"

Sinclair nodded.

"Well," he said, "it wasn't important until now. But we're taking the next step, and we're both going to find out a lot about each other — some good and some bad — so I figured why not give you the good news now."

"So does this mean you have some deep, dark secrets I'll be learning about later?" Sinclair asked, only half-joking.

"I can't promise you that I'll be perfect, Sinclair, but I can promise you that what you see is what you get. I accept you, and now all you have to do is accept me."

Ja'qazz and Sinclair stood in the middle of the living room and shared a long, silent hug. Sinclair had already surrendered herself to him, but would make him wait a while before she told him. She felt like she was finally regaining control of her life, and she didn't want to surrender that just yet, no matter how great Ja'qazz seemed to be.

Ja'qazz held tightly to Sinclair, feeling the undeniable chemistry between them. He was not a player; he had proven that when he refused the sex Aliette was practically offering up on a platter. His parents had brought him up to be respectful of women. That's not to say he didn't have his one-night stands and one-reason women, but all in all he was a one-woman man. The woman he held in his arms was his angel, and he would take care of her for the rest of his life if she would let him.

They let each other go, both feeling all tingly inside, and decided to go to dinner. It was a night to celebrate, for sure.

As they were driving, a car sped past. Sinclair recognized it as Aliette's car.

"Damn, when she drives like a bat out of hell it means she's upset about something. Maybe I should turn around and follow her," Sinclair told Ja'qazz.

"Is that what you want to do?" he asked.

"Yeah, that's what I want to do."

Ja praised Sinclair. "That's my girl." They turned the car around and caught up to Aliette's speeding car, waving her down. When she slowed, they pulled up beside her. "Follow us!" Ja yelled to Aliette.

They all went back to Sinclair's place where Aliette began crying hysterically. Her life was in turmoil, and she needed to get it together. Ever since she could remember, she had always been able to regain control. Why was this time so different? As Sinclair rubbed Aliette's back and Ja'qazz made some coffee, Aliette cried like a little girl whose best friend just moved away.

"Aliette, I'll be right back," Sinclair told her gently then went into the kitchen with Ja.

"You know, Ja, I was just thinking something," she told him.

"What is it?"

"Are you going to visit Ocean City any time soon?"

"Yeah, probably. Why?" He was starting to guess what she was thinking. He was proud she was able to still be a good friend to Aliette after everything Aliette had done to her.

"It's pretty obvious Aliette is gonna need to get away from here for a while. Maybe we could visit your bed-and-breakfast. We could all go together."

Ja hugged her. "I think that's a great idea. And I have to say, you should be proud of yourself for even giving a damn about Aliette after everything you've been through."

"Baby," Sinclair said, "I don't know where I'm getting the strength and courage to be here for her, but I just feel like I need to."

"Then be there, Sinclair. I agree with you, and we can definitely make that happen."

"It will be good for us, right? She and I can go and clear the air. Start out with a clean slate."

"Yes, baby. I think it'll be good for all of us."

"Thank you, Ja." She kissed him.

By the time Sinclair returned to the living room, Al had fallen asleep, which was just what she needed.

"Ja, please order some food," Sinclair called to him in the kitchen. "We're staying in tonight."

Chapter 25
Sun of a Beach

It was seventy-nine degrees, and the sun was beaming. As the sun's rays squeezed themselves into their pores, Sinclair and Aliette sipped on Pink Panties, a mix of gin and pink lemonade with lemon and lime wedges. The water was laughing with bursting waves, and they could hear the sound of children at play. Birds flew overhead, and the sand was hot and soft. Neither of them had to say that they were enjoying themselves. Sinclair decided the only thing missing was some music, so she turned on the two-way radio the manager had given them and requested a radio be brought to them.

A few minutes later, one of the employees brought out a boom box for their listening pleasure and refilled their glasses. While they continued to chill out, three lifeguards approached them. Both women admired their chiseled physiques as the men introduced themselves as Jonathon, Leon and DJ. They were Ja's brothers, and they worked as lifeguards at the bed-and-breakfast's private beach. Fine was an understatement, but young was written all over their faces. They advised Sinclair and Aliette that the red button on their two-way would alert the lifeguards if the women needed them. They would be at their service in a matter of seconds. Sinclair and Aliette felt like queens with their own personal lifeguards. Johnathon, Leon and DJ said good-bye and left them alone.

"Oh yeah. Talk about the life," Sinclair said. "We really need this time together, Aliette."

When she didn't receive an answer, Sinclair thought Aliette had fallen asleep, but when she looked over at Aliette, she saw streams of tears running down her face. Sinclair stared at her for a few seconds, and it reminded her of what she must have looked like the day in the park when Aliette took her picture. Sinclair reached into Aliette's bag, took her camera out and started snapping photos. She wasn't sure if Aliette heard her. If she did, she didn't say anything. Sinclair sat back down without speaking.

Aliette had seen what Sinclair was doing, but she was feeling so depressed she didn't have the strength to tell her to stop. Laying in the sun always made her tired, but this time, it had sort of paralyzed her. While her eyes were closed, she kept on imagining herself and Wayne together. Little red and blue dots danced around her eyelids then disappeared, leaving a vision of her family. That made her realize how much she missed them. For once, she felt that she needed them.

Ever since the day she left home, things hadn't been the same. Aliette would call to say hello, and it would bring back the memory of that day as if it were yesterday. That depressed her, and after a while she started calling less and less often.

Aliette's skin was burning, and the sun was drying the tears, making way for more to snake tracks down her cheeks. Aliette cried because she didn't know where to go from there. Should she pick up and totally relocate? Should she try to see if Wayne wanted to work it out? Why even consider that when she wasn't really sure she was in love with him? Her behavior toward Mia had only been in a fit of jealousy and because of a bruised ego. Aliette knew full well she hadn't loved Wayne the way he deserved to be loved in a very long time, but the fact that he had left her fueled her irrational behavior.

Aliette's stomach trembled slightly, and her breathing became choppy. She continued to cry. Sinclair continued to ignore her because she felt this was the beginning of Aliette's healing. She felt everything that happened to her had brought her to this point, and this lesson was ultimately good for her. Sinclair laid back and turned up the volume on the radio.

"That's right, y'all, this is Patrice, the Princess Pirate, holding it down for you on WIME, sizzling hot 93.5. Today we're taking calls from people who want to make amends. Whether it be with a friend or family member, give us a call so we can hook it up for ya. Come on and call. The lines are open."

Aliette jumped up and looked at Sinclair. "Oh, shit! That's my sister."

"What the hell you talking about, girl? You don't have a sister," Sinclair said, looking over at her. Aliette's tears had completely stopped now.

"Yes, Sinclair, I do. I haven't seen or heard from her in a long time. We had a really bad fight and it burned the ties between us." Her eyes teared up again. "I'm so sorry for what I did to her. I really damaged my relationships with Patrice, Manny and my mother."

"Manny? Who's that?"

"My brother."

"Aliette, we'll talk about that later, but for now, I really think you need to put a call in to the station and get the ball rolling on reconciling with your family. I can't believe you. You know, you are really fucked up. How were you able to keep this from me this long? You didn't even slip up. That's the trait of a professional liar. I'm scared of people who can do that shit." Sinclair was bringing up the same issues they had been fighting about for the last few days.

"How's it feel to be scared of yourself, Sinclair?" Aliette shot back. She was not about to let Sinclair call her a liar without admitting to her own faults in that area. "So not now with the attitude, okay?"

"Touché," Sinclair said as she handed Aliette a cell phone. "It's a local call. The station was based out of Baltimore, so get to dialing."

With sweaty palms and frayed nerves, Aliette dialed the number to the station. It was busy. She decided to keep trying until she got through. She had nothing to lose. After all, she was at what she considered to be rock bottom. A few minutes later, she tried again and got through. She gave the call screener enough information so he would put her call through to Patrice without revealing she was Patrice's sister.

"Hey now, this is Patrice, the Princess Pirate. Caller, you are on the air."

Aliette sat in silence until Sinclair nudged her with her elbow.

"Uh, hi," she said as she started to cry again. "I'm calling because I, uh, need to fix things with my sister, uh, and my family. It's been a long time since I've seen them, and the last time I did see them, we had a huge argument."

"Okay, caller. What's your name?"

Click. Aliette hung up. She was so nervous that her thumb, which she had kept near the talk button, slipped and pressed it by accident.

"Well, I guess she didn't want to reach out that bad," Patrice announced to her listeners. "Maybe she'll call back, maybe not. It's time for a break now. When I come back, I'll take some more calls."

Music started to play, and Aliette was crying again. Sinclair handed her a towel.

"Here, wipe your face. Everything will be alright. Give it a few then call back."

Aliette just fell back into her chair and remained silent. Maybe it wasn't time for her to try to contact Patrice, she thought. After a few minutes, though, she got up her nerve. She called again and got through the first time. The screener put her through to Patrice.

"Caller, who do you need to make it right with?"

"Patrice, it's your sister, Aliette. How're you doing?"

"Aliette . . ." Patrice was obviously taken aback, but recovered quickly since she was on the air. "Wow. It's been a long time."

"Yeah, I know. The time that we've been apart has made me see that family is more important than my personal needs. I was hoping we could get together and talk."

The line was silent, then suddenly there was music. The emotions that overcame Patrice forced her to put Aliette on hold. For her listeners, she pretended Aliette had been cut off again, then she announced a commercial-free block of music. She needed some time off the microphone to get her head back together.

"Hello?" Aliette spoke into the phone. She turned to Sinclair and said, "I think she put me on hold. What should I do?"

"Give her some time, Al," Sinclair advised. Aliette waited nervously for Patrice to come back to the phone.

Dang, all these years of wanting to hear from Aliette and I freeze up when I have the chance, Patrice thought.

She left Aliette on hold for a few moments because she didn't know what to say. Patrice paced around in her booth and touched the patch that covered her eye. Immediately, she was brought back to the day when Aliette cut her face. Patrice had been terrified that she would not only lose her eye, but that her face would be severely scarred. She had never been so scared in her life.

But little did Aliette know, Patrice and the rest of the family never held a grudge. They had forgiven her. When Aliette left, Patrice cried for her sister. She, at an early age, learned that it was Aliette who was the weak one and she, the strong one. The things that Aliette used to do to her only clarified this. Aliette needed her ego stroked and required all eyes on her. While Patrice fell back and let it happen, she was made stronger. She dealt with the rejection and the secondhand attention she felt she got because she knew her sister needed it more. Patrice knew the day would come when she would get hers.

Patrice cried as she finally picked up the line. "Hey, sis, how've you been?" she asked tentatively.

"Man, Patti Duke." This was what Aliette called her sister when she was feeling good after a day of being spoiled by everybody. "I'm sitting here on the beach in Ocean City with my friend, and I heard you on the radio." She took Sinclair's hand and Sinclair willingly gave it with tears in her eyes.

"I was scared to call you at first, but my friend Sinclair encouraged me. I guess I'm not as strong as I thought I was. How are things with you, Mommy and Manny? Patrice, your eye . . ." Aliette's voice faded as she remembered the horrible thing she'd done to her sister.

"My eye has been gone. Besides, I can't imagine you called me to talk about my eye. Aliette, I went through a lot of counseling because I missed you so much. Getting you back was more important than my own recuperation. Mommy told me I had to you let go. You needed to find yourself, and when you were ready, you would come back. Is it safe to assume you came back to Maryland to reconnect with us, or are you just here vacationing?"

"To tell you the truth, my life has been nothing but horrible since I left. The day I left, I went over to Daddy's house. He didn't let me stay there because I guess Mom got to him before I did and told him what had happened. But before letting me go, he gave me a piece of his mind. As usual, it went in one ear and out the other. I continued to do what I wanted to do, to whomever I wanted to do it to, and as a result, I ruined someone's marriage, I ruined my own upcoming marriage, and I feel like shit. That's it in a nutshell. So do you think we can get together while I'm here?" Aliette asked hopefully.

"When are you leaving?"

"Not until I see you. I don't care how long it takes. I'll get a job and pay rent here and wait until you're ready. I'm not leaving until I see you and the rest of the family."

Patrice wasn't sad or angry. She was overcome with a feeling of love and empathy. She had to remind herself to be careful, though. After all, her sister had hurt her so many times in the past that Patrice couldn't be one hundred percent certain this time wouldn't turn out the same way. But that didn't stop her from giving Aliette her phone number and taking hers. After all, Patrice wanted to see her sister.

The sisters disconnected their call and Sinclair just looked at Aliette, who knew that when Sinclair got that certain look in her eyes, Aliette had some explaining to do. Aliette began to tell Sinclair about the many things she had done in her youth to get attention, and the details about that horrible day, the last day she'd seen her family.

Sinclair just looked down at her feet. If Aliette only knew what Sinclair would give just to be with her mother again. The thought brought tears to her eyes. Sinclair lay back in her chair.

"Aliette, God has given you the chance to make it right with your family. That is a blessing not many people get. Don't ruin it. Take that precious gift and make amends with your family."

Aliette bent over, gave Sinclair a kiss and a hug, then reached over for the two-way radio. She ordered another pitcher of Pink Panties, and they drank until they both passed out.

A little while later, Ja'qazz, along with his parents, Mr. and Mrs. Johnson, came out to tell the women that dinner was ready. Seeing them asleep, they left them alone. They placed their hats properly on their heads and covered them with their towels. Ja'qazz kissed Sinclair on her cheek, then he and his parents returned to the house.

Shortly thereafter, the chill off the water woke Aliette and Sinclair. Groggy, they gathered their things and walked hand in hand into the house.

"I think we're gonna be okay, Al."

"I think so, too, Sin."

Ja'qazz and his parents were having cocktails in the kitchen. Sinclair took a seat next to Ja'qazz, and Aliette retreated to her room to get cleaned up. As she was entering her room, she noticed there was a message tacked to the board. It was from Patrice. She had called while Aliette was asleep on the beach and wanted her to call back when she got a chance. After Aliette had a shower, she would give her a call. It would be late, but she was going to call anyway.

Downstairs, Ja'qazz, his parents and Sinclair were talking about the house. Sinclair loved how they had decorated it and the amenities they had for their guests made them feel special. The name, The Alexis House, gave it a classier appeal.

As she made small talk with Ja's parents she wondered about the way he had introduced her to them earlier. He had told them she was his friend.

Why is he being funny now that he's in front of his parents? Maybe he just hadn't told them about me yet, she thought. She had to remember to call him on that one later.

Upstairs, Aliette called Patrice, and they agreed Patrice would meet her at the bed-and-breakfast around one o'clock the next day. When Aliette got off the phone, she joined everybody downstairs. Sinclair had already poured her a drink and had it ready when Aliette came in the room. Ja'qazz introduced her to his parents, and they sat talking about everything from soup to nuts.

The entire time, Ja'qazz was sneaking looks at Sinclair. He had a really nervous feeling, but he couldn't pinpoint what it was that was making him feel that way. He was thinking about how beautiful Sinclair was. To have her in his arms was what he wanted at that very moment. She saw him staring and looked at him curiously. They smiled at each other then chimed in on the conversation that was going on around them. He, however, was still thinking about her.

Up to this point in his life, Ja'qazz hadn't even considered having a serious relationship. The relationships that he did have prior to Sinclair didn't have a strong foundation. True, he always treated the women he dated with respect, but he'd never felt a close bond with anyone he thought might lead to something deeper than basic sex and a few good dates. The friendship had never grown, which was why the relationships never lasted.

Unfortunately, Ja was starting to realize this was the case with Sinclair also. Everything had happened so fast, and it dawned on him now that he hardly knew this woman. There had been no time for them to form a friendship, and she clearly still had some deep issues to work through. Was he willing to risk getting into a serious relationship with Sinclair at this point, especially since they were about to be business partners? He had to admit to himself that having her friendship would ultimately be more important to him than rushing into a physical relationship with her. He loved her that much.

The serious look on his face caught Sinclair's eye once again, and this time she grabbed a pencil and paper. She jotted him a note.

What's the matter with you? Why you keep looking at me like that? she wrote. She folded the paper and put it under the table. He reached under, grabbed it and read it. He excused himself, asking Sinclair if she wanted to sit on the porch with him to talk about their business venture while his parents and Aliette talked. Sinclair accepted his offer and they went outside.

They sat on a huge porch swing quietly, swaying back and forth. Sinclair wondered about his real reason for asking him outside and decided to wait for him to speak first. For a moment, Ja thought about how to say what he wanted to tell her. For fear of upsetting her, he wanted to choose his words carefully.

"Come on, I know when something's on your mind. What is it? You can talk to me," Sinclair finally said.

"Sinclair, I'm gonna come right out and say this, but I don't want you to misunderstand. So if I sound like I'm babbling, tell me if you're not following." He took a deep breath, and when she didn't speak, he continued. "Since we've met, our relationship has flourished faster than I believe we both expected."

She nodded in agreement.

"Given that, our friendship hasn't had a chance to be formed," he explained. "The time that we've spent together was beautiful. I believe the feelings that we have for each other are real. Still, I don't want to jump into a relationship with you because if it doesn't work out, then we may both be bitter."

Sinclair looked into his eyes and tried not to cry. She knew he was right, even though she had been hoping Ja'qazz could be a part of the new life she planned to start now that she was beginning to heal her past wounds. Now he was breaking up with her before they'd even really had a chance to get started. Then Ja finished his thoughts, and she knew she could have him in her life forever if she wanted.

"I don't ever want to be at odds with you, Sinclair. I don't ever want us to break up. Right now, I really don't know if you need a relationship complicating your life when you have so many other things you need to resolve. I'd rather be your friend and stand by you while you heal than have you as my girl and risk losing you someday if we break up. This doesn't mean I love you any less. In fact, I love you so much I never want to be the reason you feel grief of any kind. If I know you, I know you understand." He reached for her hand and held it gently.

"I totally understand, Ja. If I could take the physical part of our relationship and put it on the back burner, I would. I would put more effort into building our friendship, less the drama, and would slowly release my horny hormones." They both laughed. "But what we shared was special, Ja'qazz, and I don't ever want to forget it."

He took her under his arm, and they continued to swing until she fell asleep. He carried her to her room, took off her shoes and put her to bed. By then, everybody else was asleep. It was a good night for everybody.

Chapter 26
Face-to-Face

Noon came before Aliette knew it, and Patrice would be there shortly. Aliette had told Sinclair about Patrice coming, and Sinclair in turn advised Ja and his parents.   She told them Aliette was having a reunion with a sister she hadn't seen in a long time, leaving out all the ugly details of their childhood. Ja and his parents thought it was wonderful and decided to have a big lunch gathering on the beach. Sinclair tried to calm Aliette's nerves. Aliette asked for a drink.

"Aliette, you've been on a drinking binge for days now. Try being sober for this," Sinclair suggested. *Come to think of it, I've been drinking too much myself*, she thought.

"Any emotion that you feel, Aliette, should be sincere, not from the effects of a drink."

Aliette knew Sinclair was right. Her drinking was becoming out of control; it was something of which she needed to get a hold. She was letting all of her issues turn her into a drunk, but she refused to go out like that, especially now that the hard part was over. She'd made contact with Patrice.

Now, she needed to know humility. It was now that she would start taking responsibility for her actions. Today, she would start her personal healing and reformation, hopefully with Sinclair and Patrice by her side.

Sinclair and Aliette went downstairs to see if they could offer any help preparing the luncheon. Aliette went to help Jonathon and Leon put the tablecloths on the tables and set up the chairs while Sinclair, DJ and Ja folded napkins. Mr. and Mrs. Johnson sat at the dining room table and made the flower arrangements from fresh roses of different colors, with sprigs of baby's breath—Sinclair's favorite. When everything was done, the tables looked beautiful. The wine was chilling and the food was warming. Everyone stood around the tables and admired the spread.

It was at that point that everybody, including Jonathon, Leon and DJ told Aliette that she had their support. Though they didn't know why she was as nervous as she seemed, everyone had noticed how uncomfortable the whole reunion seemed to be making her. They promised to help her through this in any way she needed.

An SUV pulled up to the front of the house. Aliette felt like she was going to pass out. Mrs. Johnson saw this and signaled Sinclair to get on one side of Aliette while she got on the other. Mr. Johnson and the others stayed behind while Sinclair, Aliette and Mrs. Johnson walked toward the front of the house. Patrice stepped out of the car. She was dressed in a black-and-off-white linen suit. Her hair was pinned up with locks flowing down the sides of her face. Her eye was patched. A glossy, sheer taupe lipstick enhanced her full lips while a thin line of brown lip liner added a finished touch. Her face was flawless. As they got closer to her, Aliette felt that at any minute she would faint, so she grabbed onto Sinclair and Mrs. Johnson.

Sinclair leaned over and whispered in her ear. "I'm right here, Aliette."

Mrs. Johnson smiled and held Aliette tighter.

Patrice stopped midway to take a good look at her sister. She thought Aliette looked thin and kind of unhealthy. She could tell that Aliette wasn't taking good care of herself. Patrice walked closer to Aliette, then she started to cry. Aliette let go of Sinclair and Mrs. Johnson and ran to her sister. They embraced each other tightly.

"I've missed you so much," Patrice managed to say through her tears.

"Patrice, I'm so sorry."

Sinclair and Mrs. Johnson watched from a distance, hugging in celebration of the reunion. Aliette pulled away slightly from Patrice to get a good look at her face. She was absolutely stunning, though the sight of her eye patch brought a twinge of pain to Aliette's heart. A rattling sound came from the back of the SUV, breaking their magical moment.

The back door of the SUV electronically unfolded and a ramp was slowly lowered. The rear door on the passenger's side opened. Aliette smiled through her tears as she watched the woman getting out of the car. The woman walked around, stopped at the back of the SUV and helped a wheelchair-bound man out of the vehicle. It was Aliette's mother, Grace, and her brother, Manny. They approached the two sisters. Another set of footsteps came from around the truck, and Aliette saw her father. By then, both Patrice and Aliette had become so overwhelmed with emotions that they had to sit on the grass.

Still hugging each other, they watched their mother wheel Manny over while their father followed. Their parents sat next to them, each taking a side, and embraced their children. Joy filled the air, and faces showed happiness, sorrow, humility, forgivenes, and last but not least, love.

Sinclair and Mrs. Johnson went to the beach area to give Aliette and her family some privacy. The family sat together and prayed. They thanked God for this day, for bringing Aliette back home, no matter how many bricks she had to lay to make the road for her to get there, for the love that they shared even after being separated for that long period of time, for friends and for family.

Chapter 27
Roundtable #2

Brunch was very nice. Everyone kept the conversation light, and everyone had a good time. Aliette couldn't take her eyes off Patrice. How could her sister continue to love her after all the harm she had caused? Aliette knew she was blessed to have her family back, and she promised she wouldn't do anything to cause problems in their relationship again.

Patrice had excused herself from the table. Since her injury, she had to put drops in her eye often to prevent it from drying out. Aliette asked if she needed company, but Patrice told her no. Mrs. Johnson asked Aliette how she felt now that she'd had such a happy reunion with her family.

"Mrs. Johnson, why I've been given another chance to love and be loved by my family is beyond me. I've done some very selfish things in my life," Aliette admitted, "and I feel very sorry for hurting the people who love me. For a long time, I didn't know who I was, and I'm still trying to figure that out. I know that no one can help me do that, but it would feel mighty good to know that I have support from my friends and family." She looked at her brother and her parents. Though she was still talking to Mrs. Johnson, her message was really meant for her family. She wanted them to understand why she had acted the way she had when she was younger, hoping they could forgive her now.

"My parents split up when I was thirteen. I was really close to my father. He and I used to talk about everything. Any time I was lonely, he would play with me. Any time I wanted something to eat, he would either cook it for me or take me out to eat. When my father moved out, it was like someone took my heart and squeezed all the love out of it. That's when I started acting up.

"At first, I looked for my brother to be my rock. When he developed his own relationship with Patrice, I took it very personally. He was the second man who had, what I considered at the time, abandoned me." Her father lowered his head and began to cry. Aliette continued.

"My mother's name fits her perfectly. Everything she said was spoken with grace, and everything she did was done that way too. She taught me how to sew, cook and do my hair, and that ladies don't always have to have a glass when drinking beer, as long as you cross your legs when you tip the bottle back." This made everyone at the table laugh.

"Everybody was there for me, but it wasn't good enough. I did everything I could to get the attention I wanted, and I didn't care who was hurt in the process. As a result of my selfishness, my sister lost an eye, and probably has had many nights where she cried herself to sleep. My brother, who was shot in crossfire and is confined to a wheelchair, received no sympathy from me." Manny looked over at her.

"I'm sorry, Manny, for trying to make you choose between me and Patrice."

He reached across the table and squeezed her hand. He accepted her apology, though he had forgiven her long ago.

"My mother, who has always tried to right everybody's wrongs, had to deal with an ungrateful child. With all that, I probably would have put me out too." Aliette hung her head low and lived her first true moment of humility.

Everyone at the table was silent. Then Manny wheeled himself over to Aliette's side and spoke. "Al, I'm not gonna tell you that you're being too hard on yourself. I will tell you this, though. We all were well aware that out of the three of us, you needed to be the center of attention. Really, there was nothing wrong with that. But we didn't know how to make you understand that we loved you no matter what.

"Did you even know that all you had to do was ask Patrice to borrow something of hers and she would have given it to you? Were you remotely aware of the fact that if I had listened to you and not gone out with those knuckleheads I could have walked to you today instead of being wheeled by Mommy? Did it ever occur to you that our parents needed time to themselves and that Daddy couldn't come every time you rang your silver bell? It took so much from everybody that we eventually just existed — not as a family, but a group of people who lived under the same roof. But as grim as it may seem, this was our plan, and we just have to accept it."

Grace spoke. "When Patrice told us that you had contacted her, it was like coming out of darkness. Families have problems, but when you lose a child behind those problems, you're not the same. It is so easy to learn anger and spite. Society says to stand up for what you believe in. We claim to believe in our families, but are very quick to judge them. We all love you, and we're glad you have come home."

Aliette got up and gave her parents and brother a hug. Ja's parents, Sinclair and Ja'qazz got up and joined the group hug.

Aliette noticed Patrice hadn't returned yet, so she went to find her. The light was on in the hall bathroom, so she assumed Patrice was in there. She slowly pushed the door open. Patrice had just finished washing her face and was now drying it. Unaware that Aliette was in the bathroom, she removed the towel from her face. For the first time, Aliette saw her sister's eye without the patch. Patrice looked at her through the mirror and neither of them moved. Finally, Patrice turned around so she could look at Aliette face-to-face. Aliette's insides were cramping as she felt a rush of great shame. Patrice walked over to her, took her hand and placed it on her eye. Aliette didn't pull back.

"I'm so sorry, Patrice. Please forgive me."

Patrice embraced Aliette. She kissed her face. They cried and held each other tight. For the rest of the day, where there was one, the other was close behind.

Chapter 28
Friends by Accident

The drive home was quiet. Sinclair sat in the front with Ja'qazz while Aliette retreated to the back. Sinclair was thinking about all that had happened.

"I don't know about you guys, but I feel like I'm a different person." She laid her head on the headrest. "All these months of drama actually had a purpose in the end."

Aliette spoke. "For the last couple of weeks my body has been functioning normally in that I can walk, I can talk, I can hear and see, but I feel like my mind has been strait-jacketed in a padded room." She rubbed her temples and continued. "Since I can remember, I've had to have my way. Instead of treating people the way I demanded to be treated, I dogged them every chance I got. I was so used to feeling alone."

"But you weren't alone, Aliette," Ja said. "I don't understand."

"Me neither. I was an unhappy, never-satisfied child," Aliette admitted.

"Has anything changed about your family, Aliette? Have they always shown you love like that?" Sinclair asked.

"Mm-hmm." Aliette nodded.

"But it wasn't enough?"

"No."

"Maybe you had too much. I wish I could see my mother again. You take for granted what you have, and sometimes you have to lose it to know how important it was to you."

"I know that now."

Sinclair turned around to face Aliette and asked, "Do you really?"

Ja'qazz looked at Aliette through the rearview mirror.

Aliette swallowed hard and said, "Yes."

The drive home was serene. Aliette got dropped off first, then Ja'qazz drove Sinclair home.

"Well, see you first thing tomorrow morning, partner," Ja said.

"You got it," Sinclair responded as she leaned over and gave him a kiss on the cheek.

It was obvious their purpose for each other was greater than either of them had imagined it would be. For Sinclair, who hadn't felt confident about her inner self and sexuality in a long time, he had redefined her womanhood. He reminded her that she was whole and worthy of a good love.

For Ja'qazz, Sinclair had taught him something about women. She was unique. Just because someone comes in a pretty package doesn't mean that what's in her heart is pretty too. But Sinclair, even for all her issues, was beautiful outside and inside. She had been through some terrible heartache in her life, but she had managed to maintain her self-respect. The way Sinclair had helped Aliette, the woman who had ruined her marriage, taught Ja the true meaning of friendship and love.

Ja'qazz gave Sinclair a hug, and she received it. They held each other, knowing that what they shared was beautiful, a memory that would be a part of them forever.

"So," Ja said before he pulled away, "can I get the office with the bay window?"

"But of course."

Back in Maryland

"Well, listeners, I gotta tell you about my weekend. I was reunited with my sister who I haven't seen in years. The terms in which we parted were horrible, but now that we've seen each other and talked, we're back on even ground. We made a promise that we would see each other every month. We're going to meet up at The Alexis House and get to know each other all over again while we resolve all our old pains. I have to say it feels good! Give me a call. The lines are open. Tell me if there's anyone you need to be friends with again, whether it's a family member, or maybe even yourself. This is Patrice the Princess Pirate, and I'm waiting for your call."